Southern Betrayal

Southern Secrets: Book Two

by
ABEL OZUNA

Southern Secrets: Book Two

Table of Contents

Sign up for Abel's newsletter and get a FREE book today!

http://abelozuna.com/newsletter

* * *

Follow Abel on social media:

Twitter: http://twitter.com/abelozuna4

Facebook: http://facebook.com/abelozuna04

Instagram: http://instagram.com/abelozuna4

Snapchat: abeloiv

Southern Secrets: Book Two

Prologue

A few months ago the world as I knew it, changed. I am a Sheer, my girlfriend is a Fae, my best friend is a vampire, and werewolves exist. The scary stories I was told as a kid have all come true.

The person I thought was responsible for killing my parents, turned out to be my own dad. Yeah, I know. He never actually died. Malute, who was once a Sheer, has turned evil and wants to rid the earth of all supernaturals except his version of the Sheer, which he calls the Shyne.

After he killed my ex-girlfriend, who was a werewolf, kidnapped my best friend and killed my new girlfriend's dad, he had the balls to ask me to join him in his

1

mission to get rid of the 'ungodly' creatures from this realm. Yeah, right. Like that's gonna happen.

When Malute told me that I was his son, in true Mason form, I immediately passed out. Maw and the others were finally able to break through his wards as he dematerialized with his sidesick, Avant.

I'm going to find him, and this time he should be extremely afraid of me. Now that my full Sheer powers are intact, when we meet, I'm going to kill him — even if he is my dad.

1.

I was getting ready to meet with Layla, when my phone started to ring. I checked the caller ID and then answered.

"Hello? Mimaw? How's it going back home?"

"Ah, sweetie, it's so good to hear your voice. I'm doing alright, I just got home from a council meeting. I miss you. When are you all coming back home?"

As I left, I locked the door to Benjy's new apartment. "I'm not sure, really. I don't have school again until the middle of January, Maw. You know why we're here. I can't leave until I find him."

3

She stayed quiet for a minute. "I know, y'all have lots to do in Dallas. I wish that we could have stayed there, too. We are going insane knowing that Geoffrey, Benjy and the Smithwick brothers are the adults in charge. I know how crazy they can get."

I laughed, "They're in charge, but we're definitely the more responsible ones around here."

"My point exactly. Well, alright sweetie, I better be going. I'm going to the Wrightpresses' for dinner. We'll be up there in a couple of weeks for Christmas."

"I can't wait, see you soon. Tell Mrs. Wrightpress I said 'Hi'."

"Alright, will do. Give everyone a hug for me."

I hung up the phone as Layla walked up to me from down the hall. "Hey there, hot stuff."

"Hey there, sugar plum."

She laughed as Mackenna walked up. "Y'all are seriously grossing me the hell out. We're in Dallas, for God's sake, let's go get into some trouble!"

I grinned at her. "Hey, where's Tyler?"

Mack let out an annoyed sound. "Ugh, he went with Geoffrey and Benjamin to the mall. He wanted some disgusting new shoes. I told him I refused to go with him to make a bad decision, hence the reason I'm here and he's not. They're going to meet us at some restaurant later."

Great, I'm alone with Mackenna and Layla? This should be tons of fun. We drove around town for a bit, stopping by a nail salon so Mackenna could get her nails filled.

She sipped on her iced coffee while we were at a red light. "That lady did such an amazing job. I wish I could like, take her home and keep her as my personal nail tech."

Layla and I let out a roar of laughter as Layla's phone rang. She quickly picked it up, "Hello, Mom?"

After listening for some time, she said said, "Okay, well, why don't you go to Mimaw's? I will see if Mack and I can get down to help you pack up next week."

Mackenna looked at Layla with concern in her eyes. Layla hung up her phone. "My mom is having a really bad day. She was packing some stuff up for the move and had a breakdown when she got to my dad's stuff."

I grabbed her hand and squeezed it tightly. "Maw said she was going to head over there later, so at least your mom will have company." Layla leaned in and kissed me.

An hour or so later we met up with Geoffrey, Benjy and Tyler at a restaurant called Smooches. As we pulled up to the restaurant, Mackenna let out a long, exaggerated sigh. "I know Tyler picked this place. He's been trying this whole romance thing and he just doesn't give up."

Layla laughed. "I really hope the food here is better than the name."

We got out of the car and Mackenna added, "Oh, cuz, I doubt anything is going to be good here."

We all sat in a large booth towards the back of the dark restaurant and talked about the kind of day we had. After we had been there a while, Jayland ran into the restaurant. "For God's sake, do none of you ever look at your cell phones?"

We all glanced at our phones together as Geoffrey giggled, "Oops, sorry."

Jayland sat next to me, trying to catch his breath. "There's been another pack of wolves killed. Just a few miles from here."

We all stopped laughing. I asked what everyone was thinking, "Was it Malute and Avant?"

Jayland looked at me. "Ah, I wish it were just them."

Mackenna yelled out, "What the hell do you mean *just them*?"

He looked at all of us. "Y'all should get your food to go. Malute's little army of imbeciles have crossed into our realm."

My friends and I left all of our food on the table and ran out of the restaurant. I yelled out, "Jayland, we'll follow you to where the attack was. Where are your brothers?"

"They're already over there. Y'all keep up with me, we need to get there fast. I'm hoping they've picked up a scent."

II.

The drive to the place of the attack only took us about half an hour from the restaurant. We pulled up to the house and saw Marcus and Royce sitting outside with a group of men. I jumped out of the car. "Hey Royce, Marcus. What's going on? How do y'all know the realm has been opened?"

The brothers didn't have time to speak as Jayland immediately hollered at us. "Mason! You need to come and see this!"

I joined him and the rest of my friends behind the house and saw sinkholes throughout the entire cornfield. I groaned, "Holy crap."

Mackenna threw her hands up. "Great, now we have a bunch of wannabe Malutes running around Dallas?"

Geoffrey and Benjy looked at each other while Jayland rubbed his forehead with his hand. "I think the council should hear about this. What do y'all think?"

Geoffrey responded as he held up his ringing phone. "I'm pretty sure they know all about it."

He answered his phone on speaker. "Hello? I'm assuming you are calling because of what we just found."

"The sinkholes, is this true? Maw got a call from some Sheers in Dallas. They're saying crazy things, Geoffrey. Please tell me that the realm to Sinara has not been opened." Mrs. Wrightpress said anxiously.

For a few seconds Geoffrey didn't speak. "I'm sorry. I'm afraid it's true. We just got here and it's not looking good. The whole field is covered with sinkholes in it; the entire area has to be at least two miles across."

There was silence from the other end of Geoffrey's phone until Benjy spoke up. "Mrs. Wrightpress, are you with Mimaw now?"

Mrs. Wrightpresses' startled voice responded. "Yes Benjy, I am. Would you like to speak with her?"

Benjy winced. "Eh, no it's okay. Can you tell her to try not to freak out. Mason and I will head to meet with some of the local Sheers in the morning."

"Okay Benjamin, that sounds good. I will talk with you all later. Take care of my baby!".

We started walking through the field when we heard the dreaded noise from my nightmares. BANG! BANG! We all came to attention, and instantly were in a fighting stance.

Tyler screamed out, "Come out and play, you coward! We're ready!"

An eerie laugh came from the bottom of one of the sinkholes. "You fools think I'm a coward? No, no, children. I am no coward, I'm a smart man whose army is waiting for his command."

We all looked at each other and I yelled out, "You've got two things wrong, Dad. You're not smart, and you're definitely not a man. If you were a real man, you wouldn't have killed my mom. Remember her? Your wife?"

Tears were streaming down my face as the train-like sounds blared out again,

BANG! BANG! Whoa, I thought, fight it, Mase, it's happening again."

I started to feel dizzy when I heard his eerie voice in my head, "Mason, you will not disrespect me again. You have no idea what happened that night and until you do, shut your mouth! The realm is opened and I have my army of Shyne here. Will you join us?"

I screamed out, "Your army of Shyne? Where are they hiding? What in the hell are Shyne?"

BANG! BANG!

He answered me, "The Shyne are my children. They're like your dear friend, Avant. They are a mixture of all the bloodlines. They will be indestructible. Trust me when I say, you do not want to be on the wrong side of this fight Mason."

The dizziness I was experiencing was starting to really get to me when Malute spoke again. "Mason, I will come to you in your sleep. Do not fight it. We need to talk and I can't have you passing out on me, again."

"I don't think you should waste your time. I'm not leaving my friends and Mimaw to join you and those bastards. They're not your children, they're your experiments. What are you going to do when they turn their backs on you? You can only be the highest thing on the food chain for so long. And if they don't kill you, I will."

His spooky laugh flooded my head. "You're more like your pathetic mother than I thought. Until next time, Son."

BANG! BANG!

III.

I opened my eyes and saw Tyler, Layla and Mackenna all staring down at me. After a couple silenced seconds, Tyler asked, "Are you okay, Mase? What happened?"

I put my hand over my eyes to block out the sun as Tyler reached for my other hand to help me up from the ground. "I don't know. Malute said that the Shyne are here and…"

Before I could finish, Benjy cut me off. "That's impossible…the Shyne are an extinct creature. They are an abomination."

I shrugged my shoulders. "I'm glad someone has heard of them. Malute said they are his children and he was asking me to join them."

Mackenna scoffed, "I hope you told him to burn in hell." Everyone let out a small laugh as Tyler and I stared at the burnt ground.

We started walking back to the front of the house when a pair of guys came towards us.

One of them greeted us with a wave. "Hello. Which of you are the Fitzgeralds?"

Benjy and I walked towards them with our hands up. The redheaded guy smiled. "Hello, I'm Ashton Hood. This is my brother, Aden. We're a part of the local council. Mrs. Fitzgerald called us to catch us up on the recent events."

The blond guy, Aden, shook my hand and then said, "Dude, you've got some seriously strong Sheer powers. How do you have your full powers intact at such a young age? You know what, don't even answer that. I forget you're a Fitzgerald."

The brothers looked at each other as Jayland, Royce and Marcus walked up to us.

Jayland cleared his throat. "I hate to break up the little non-family reunion but what in the hell are we going to do about the Shyne?"

The Hood brothers screamed out, "The Shyne? That's impossible. They are extinct from this realm. They only exist in Sinara."

I looked back at them, "Sorry, guys. It's true. I was telling my friends about what just happened. Malute said that they're his children and then referred to them as his army."

Jayland sighed, "Okay, I'm sick of hearing this story and not doing anything about it. My brothers and I are going to see if we can catch a scent anywhere near here. Keep your phones on and I'll keep in touch."

After the Smithwick brothers left us, the Hoods joined my friends and I inside the home where the werewolves were murdered. We walked into the master bedroom and Layla cried out, "What the hell happened here?"

Geoffrey coughed while covering his mouth in disgust. "This poor pack was slaughtered."

Benjy spoke up from the other side of the room, where he was standing with the

Hood brothers, "Hey y'all, come here. Avant left us a little message."

We walked over to the guys. Layla grabbed my hand and whispered, "Mason, we need to catch these things, fast."

I nodded as Aden prepared to read the note out loud, "You all ready?" We all looked at each other and then nodded.

He went on, "'Children of the night, moon, light and shadows. Malute and I would like to introduce you to the children of darkness. The Shyne have returned from Sinara and soon, we will be the only children walking this realm.'"

Mackenna laughed out loud. "He's got to be kidding. There's no way in hell these things will be able to get rid of us all. We're way too strong."

Geoffrey, Benjy, Aden and Ashton stayed quiet. Benjy spoke now, "Mackenna, I'm not sure you understand how strong the Shyne are. They're all going to be like Avant. They'll probably be able to dematerialize just like he can."

Layla gasped, "How do they all have the same powers? One has to be weaker than the other."

Ashton looked at her and then slowly answered her question. "I'm not sure that's true. If Malute resurrected their kind with the same blood he created Avant with, they're going to all be equal. If any of them were weak, I'm sure Malute would've killed them off by now. I don't think there's a weak link."

Benjy and Geoffrey held each other's hands when Geoffrey asked him, "Do you think your ancestors will be able to help us from the other side?"

Benjy sighed. "I sure hope so."

Mackenna spoke again, "Okay you guys, what the hell are we going to do about these things? We have to come up with a solid plan. How do we kill them? I am sick of being in limbo and just going with the flow."

Geoffrey added, "I can't believe I'm saying this, but I agree with Mack. Mason, what do you think we should do?"

Before I could answer him, my phone's text message alert went off. Mackenna asked, "Is it Jayland? Did they find Avant or Malute?"

I read the text out loud, "'Mase, we picked up on Avant's scent. It led us to an abandoned warehouse on 76th Street. Meet us here now, J'."

Benjy looked at Ashton and Aden. "You guys heading out with us?" The brothers looked at each other and nodded.

I let out a sigh of relief, "Let's go try and kill us some Shyne."

IV.

It took us about fifteen minutes to get to 76th Street. When we pulled up to the warehouse, Jayland and his brothers were standing outside, waiting for us. Tyler and I were the first out of the car. I greeted Jayland. "Hey man. Have you all gone in? Have you found anything?"

Jayland shook his head. "Nah, we can't get through the doors. They're all locked and we tried to kick them in but we went flying back every time."

Marcus let out a roar of laughter. "Yeah, there are some wards up, for sure. You should've seen Royce get tossed on his butt. It was pretty funny."

Royce, who was now sitting on the curb, added, "Yeah, keep laughing. When I recover I'm going to kick your…"

Ashton cut Royce off in the middle of his sentence, "…Did you all say that there were wards up? How did they get those up without a Sheer's help?"

We all looked at each other and Benjy answered. "Well, Malute is kind of a Fitzgerald."

Aden exclaimed, "You have got to be kidding me! How is that possible?"

Mackenna butted in, "Okay, let's not get into that. It's this long story none of us have time for. Just know, he is a Sheer, or was, and we have got to get in there. If he has the wards up he has to be in there, right?" She looked at Benjy and I for confirmation.

I shrugged. "I really don't know. I mean, if the Shyne are his supposed children, don't you think some of them may have picked up a skill or two from their Daddy?"

Ashton said, "If they did, we've got some serious problems."

Aden added, "The Sheers on the spirit realm are probably going batshit crazy right now."

Benjy laughed at the thought of our ancestors running around on the other side. "Oh, I'm sure they are."

We all started walking towards the doors, where the wards were visible to Benjy, Aden, Ashton and I. We looked at each other with concern and then turned our attention to the others.

Mackenna dropped Tyler's hand and asked, "What's going on now? Why are y'all staring at us like that?"

I stayed quiet and let Ashton answer her, "Well, these barriers are definitely Sheer wards but, um…"

Aden continued, "What my brother is trying to say is that these wards are going to take us a bit longer than normal to get through. A normal Sheer's wards are a silver color, and these are black."

Ashton added on, "They are black as night."

Benjy corrected him, "They're as dark as night."

Geoffrey clapped his hands together. "Okay, well this sucks. Let's get those dark wards down, shall we?"

Benjy smiled at his boyfriend, kissed him and then looked at us. "We're going to have to work together."

He turned to Mackenna. "That means you too, little Fae. We're gonna need that little flame power of yours."

Aden's eyes lit up with excitement. "You're a fire elemental?"

Mackenna smiled at him as she snapped her fingers together and showed off a small flame. "I sure am, so watch what you say to me. I may just burn that pretty blond hair of yours."

He laughed and snapped a silver mist from his fingers. "I'd like to see you try."

Tyler took his stance next to Mackenna and put an end to their conversation. "Okay. Enough with the chatter, let's get to work."

Layla giggled and whispered to me, "I think someone is a little jealous."

I leaned down, kissed her forehead and let out a laugh of my own. "Yeah, Ty looks pretty annoyed."

I stood next to Benjy, Ashton and Aden. No one said a word as we all stared at the wards. I finally asked, "So, where the hell do we even start?"

Benjamin put his hand on my shoulder. "Cousin, I wish I knew."

Aden spoke up, "We should all try to project our powers towards the wards."

Geoffrey looked at Mackenna and Layla, and added, "While y'all are doing that, we can use our affinities to attack the dark wards." The girls nodded in agreement.

Tyler and the Smithwick brothers stood next to each other. Jayland spoke, "When we start to see the wards, the four of us can use our strength to break through them and get to the door."

Mackenna huffed. "It's about time we had a plan. Are y'all ready to break into this joint?"

We all grinned at one another as Benjy, Aden, Ashton and I lifted our palms. I closed my eyes and mumbled, "I, Mason, of the Fitzgerald bloodline call upon my ancestors. Help us take down these dark wards."

A few seconds later, my palms were vibrating and a bright silver mist shot out of them and towards the ward. The second it touched the ward, I was thrown back violently. I kept my palms up and kept them facing the dark wall as

Benjamin and the Hood brothers joined me.

Ashton exclaimed, "You guys, we've got to give it everything we've got!"

Benjy responded, "Uh, I don't know about you all, but I kind of am!"

We focused on pouring our silver mist into the dark wards as I felt something strange happening in my palms. There was a burning sensation running through my fingertips. I looked over at Benjamin who was now breaking out in a sweat. I called out, "Benjy, you don't feel that? It's burning me!"

He looked at me, confused, but before he could answer I heard one of my ancestors. "Mason, we're here. We've never seen anything like these dark wards. We're going to channel our energy through you and it is going to feel quite unpleasant."

I nodded and heard Benjamin's distant voice. "Mason, what are you doing?"

I opened my eyes and saw that my Sheer mist was turning white and then noticed that it started looked like a bunch of tidal waves slamming into the darkness. I suddenly felt the fire sensation run through my entire body. *Crap, my head is hurting! If y'all on the other side can hear me, please make it stop! I can't last much longer.*

The familiar voice stated, "You can do it Mason. You all must break the wards. Tell your Fae friends to start working with their affinities. The dark wards are very close to breaking."

I opened my eyes and looked back at the Wrightpresses. "Geoffrey, y'all start, now!"

Geoffrey, Layla and Mackenna took their stances next to me. I felt Mackenna's heat,

Geoffrey's air and Layla's misty water. I looked at Layla. "Give it all you've got. We're close!"

She winked at me. "I always do."

A second later my ancestor's voice was back. "Tell the others to start going towards the ward. It is about to start cracking next to the Hoods."

I nodded. "Tyler, we're ready for y'all. Go full force, man."

Tyler's chest rose with pride. "Yeah, yeah, yeah. Just tell me where to push."

I pointed at the small gap in between Ashton and Aden. Tyler and the Smithwick brothers stepped back and then ran towards the opening.

The guys broke through the wards and we were all sent flying back. I hit the ground and felt myself fall into unconsciousness. My ancestor's voice came through, "Mason, you did it! You've broken through the dark wards. You have impressed us all, my child. Now go in and take care of those creatures!"

V.

When I opened my eyes, everyone was getting up. Tyler hovered over me and held out his hand. "Bro, you should have seen your face!"

I gave him an ugly stare-down as I stood up. "Oh really? Am I the only one who made a weird face?"

We looked around as Mackenna was wiping her hands on her jeans. "Tyler, instead of worrying about Mason's face, why aren't you over here helping me up?"

Tyler sprinted towards her. "Sorry, babe."

She pushed him away and hit him on the shoulder. Geoffrey and Benjamin cleared their throats. Geoffrey spoke, "I've had enough from you annoying kids, settle down."

Benjy pointed at the broken door. "Look, you guys, we did it. We got the wards down."

Jayland walked up to us with Royce and Marcus trailing him. "I guess we do make a pretty good team, huh? Who would have thought, Wrightpresses and Smithwicks working together? I'll be damned."

Geoffrey's facial expression was one of disgust as Ashton spoke. "Hey y'all, I think that we should go in first." He pointed at Aden, Benjamin and I and then went on, "If there are any Shyne in the lower part of the building they won't be able to detect us right away."

Mackenna and Tyler were about to protest but Jayland and Geoffrey nodded in agreement. Geoffrey explained, "I think that idea is best. If a Shyne detects anyone, it would be one of us first."

Mackenna huffed, "Don't you think our affinities would be a little helpful in fighting them off from a distance?"

Benjamin answered, "Your affinities with the elements would definitely help but I think that Mason is pretty much a vessel connected to the other side right now. We're pretty powerful at the moment."

Jayland added, "Alright, so you Sheers go in first, then we'll follow with little vamp. Wrightpresses, I think since you all aren't going in first, it's best if you all go in last. You'll be able to guard our backs while the Sheers are in the front. We'll be here for muscle power, but the Shyne have to

let us get close enough to them for us to
be of any help."

Layla, Mackenna and Geoffrey nodded as
we heard the dreaded noise. **BANG!**
BANG! Without hesitating, we all ran
into the warehouse.

VI.

The moment we entered the building, we were confronted by a horrendous stench. Mackenna's voice came from the back of the group. "God, what is that smell?"

"I don't know. It smells like someone freaking died in here," Geoffrey added.

Ashton and Aden answered before Benjamin could. "It's the Shyne, they're here. Mason, can you sense them?"

I closed my eyes and let my ancestors' powers travel through my body. My eyes flew open and we followed the white mist that was spilling from my hands.

Benjamin stayed close to me. I heard him tell Geoffrey, "Babe, be careful and take care of the girls. These things are strong."

We made our way deeper into the warehouse and stopped when the mist retracted back into my palms. Tyler was standing behind me when he asked, "Do you think we need to go upstairs now?"

I shook my head in confusion. Jayland came up to us as his brothers stayed closer to the Wrightpresses. He whispered to us, "I don't smell anything now, what about you two?"

Tyler and I looked at each other and Jayland sighed. "I didn't think so." He turned his attention to the Hood brothers. "What do you all think we should do now? Sit here and wait?"

Ashton answered. "No, I think we need to split up."

Mackenna said, "Like hell we do. I don't think that splitting up is a good idea. If we're all together, we're a lot stronger than they are."

"I don't know if that's true. I don't think any of the Shyne will appear if we stay together. Maybe we should split up in small groups. One Sheer, one Fae, and on Were in each group?" Aden responded to Mackenna.

Before anyone could agree to the plan, we heard **BANG! BANG!** We all circled around each other, looking nervously.

I yelled out, "Come out and play, you cowards!"

A second later, Malute's voice was in my head again. "Mason, my dear son. Haven't you learned that I do not like to be called a coward?"

I fought off the light-headed sensation, I had no time to pass out, and I forced myself to channel my ancestors' powers. *Man, I'm getting pretty good at this.* "Haven't you learned that I don't care what you like? Why do you keep playing hide and seek with me? I don't want to play games anymore, come out and face me like the man you claim to be!" I yelled.

He let out an eerie laugh. "Oh, you fool."

I looked at my friends who were all looking at me. A violet orb came flying from the stairs and landed between Geoffrey and Benjamin. I screamed out, "Are you all okay?"

Benjamin leaped up and nodded his head as he helped Geoffrey back to his feet.

Layla yelled out now, "Malute, I swear to God, we are going to kill you!"

Malute laughed again. "My son, tell your little Fae girlfriend to watch her mouth. She does not want to upset me."

Layla met my eyes. I signaled for her to be quiet. "Malute, what are you waiting for? Why have you not just come out and taken over the world like the big bad man that you are? You said when your Shyne were here you'd be ready, and I don't know if you got the memo or not, but they're here."

Malute grunted. "Mason, I will execute my plan when I am ready. I do not need to explain myself to you or any of your filthy excuse for friends." He continued, "But you are right about one thing, my Shyne are here. They are waiting for me to release them into the world. I've got to tell you, they're very anxious to meet you. Why don't you go upstairs and say hello to some of them? I'll see you soon, son."

My friends and I tightened our circle and I spoke first. "Were you all able to hear him this time?"

Everyone nodded. Their eyes showed they felt as confused as I did. "Let's get up there and show these Shyne they're messing with the wrong people. What do y'all say?" Ashton said.

We rearranged ourselves into the groups we'd decided on, and then we headed upstairs.

VII.

As we made our way up the stairs the smell we'd noticed when we first arrived came back, full force. We all started gagging and a couple of seconds later, Mackenna leaned over and threw up.

Layla held her cousin's hair back while Mackenna screamed at Tyler. "For God's sake Tyler. You should be the one helping me, not my cousin. Don't you know how to be a decent boyfriend?"

Tyler ran to her side, nervously. "Uh, sorry, babe. You know this is all a little new to me. I'm learning though, right?"

Mackenna glared at him. Layla handed her a bottle of water and whispered,

"Come on Mackenna. We've got to keep going."

After a few more minutes of Mackenna's sickness, Layla started to use her air affinity to get rid of some of the smell – for which we were all really grateful.

We finally made it to the to third floor when we saw *them*. Three tall, skinny figures with bloodshot eyes. They were all smiling at us, revealing their razor sharp teeth. The thing standing in the middle spoke, "Ah, I'm glad you all made it here. What took you so long?" The creature licked its dry, cracked lips and I suddenly felt sick again.

I spit out at it. "Why are you three sitting up here like little pets? Is that what you are to Malute? His little pets?"

The Shyne in the middle smiled again. "Ah, Avant told us you would be filled with resentment towards our father."

I shouted, "He is not my father, he's the damned devil!"

The Shyne that stood to the left pointed his index fingers to the floor. "The devil? Oh, no dear boy. The devil of Sinara himself is afraid of Malute, as he should be."

Mackenna laughed. "I've had enough of this." She snapped her fingers and held a fireball in her hand. She looked at Layla and Geoffrey. "Are you two ready to play?"

We all took our stance and braced ourselves for whatever power the Shyne may have ready to throw at us.

The Shyne who looked to be in charge threw a violet orb at us. We easily dodged out of its path. I.held out my palms and let my silver mist surround them.

Tyler and the Smithwick brothers circled the three Shyne as we knocked them to their feet. Ashton and Aden held them down while I stood over them.

I smiled back at them, as they had done to us. "Is this all you've got?" I asked.

They spit at me.

I let the mist turn from a bright silver to a dark gray and covered their mouths with it. They started choking. "Please, don't piss me off. Where are Malute and Avant? If you tell us where they are, I'll think about letting you live."

They let out muffled laughter. I released the mist from one of their mouths. "We are immortal, like our father. We cannot be killed."

I glanced at Benjy and the Hood brothers for back-up. They let their silver mist surround the Shyne, squeezing them tightly. They started to squirm and make howling noises.

Jayland snarled, "Oh no. We're the only things that howl around here, boys." He bit into one of the Shyne's necks and blackened blood spewed out.

Mackenna covered her mouth with one hand while she tossed a small fireball at the Shyne's feet.

The Shyne on the right cried out, "Okay, Okay. Stop, I'll tell you where Father is!"

We all stood still while the Shyne looked at each other anxiously. From their expressions it was clear they had decided to talk but the second leader open its mouth, flames appeared and covered them; within seconds the fires were burning out of control. Unable to do anything, we watched as the intensity increased until all three Shyne exploded, and we were all showered in their boiling black blood.

We all fell back, disgusted. Tyler spoke up, "This is gross. Mack, why did you have to blow them up?"

Mackenna grunted and gave Tyler a disapproving look. "Tyler, do not talk to me right now. I didn't set the damn things on fire. And you know what? Don't bother coming near me today. You're really on my last nerve. I have billions of nerves in my body and you are now on every single one of them."

Tyler put his hands in his pockets while the rest of the group cleaned themselves off.

As we all started to regain our composure, we heard the loud train-like noise blare from somewhere inside the abandoned warehouse. **BANG! BANG!**

I looked at my friends as Geoffrey spoke, "Oh God, not again."

Mackenna and Layla shrieked as Tyler, Ashton, Aden and the Smithwicks flew into the air.

Tyler screamed, "Mason, help me. Make him stop!"

I started running around the room and shouted at Benjy and the Wrightpresses. "Do y'all see anyone?" The girls ran to the door as Geoffrey and Benjamin ran up the stairs.

Geoffrey screamed out, "Mason, get up here. Get up here, now!"

I ran towards the fourth floor when I heard Tyler and the Hood brothers cry out in pain.

The minute I got to the top of the stairs, my insides seemed to freeze up. Layla shouted from the third floor, "Mason, I think all of the guys are passed out, I mean, I think they're okay, I-I just don't know about the Smithwicks!"

I held my breath for a minute and listened. Jayland cried out from the floors beneath us, "Royce, Marcus, get up, please!"

Benjy looked at me and then pointed at the disgusting things standing in front of us. There had to be more than a hundred of the Shyne standing still, not breathing. As if they were all in stand-by mode.

"It's like they're in some kind of trance," Geoffrey whispered.

Before I could say anything, Avant shouted from the top floor. "We meet again, Mason."

VIII.

We all looked at each other and I started to run up the next flight of stairs. Avant let out a creepy laugh. "Ah, ah, ah. I wouldn't take another step if I were you."

I stood still for a second. "Why not? Why are all these Shyne just sitting here?"

I heard footsteps walking down, towards me. A second later Avant was in front of me. "Mason, it is so good to see you again. I see you've made some new friends."

I stepped back. "I wish I could say the same for you. I have a couple more Sheers with me, so if I were you I'd watch your next step."

Avant tiptoed and looked over my shoulders. "Oh my, you've got the Hood brothers here? I'm sure they'll love to know I'm here."

I spit out. "They do know you're here. Now, enough with the banter. Why are you here? Why are the Shyne here? Where is Malute?"

Avant raised an eyebrow as he came closer to me. He shook his head. "No questions, Mason. You all are brave to come to our lair. How did you find us?"

I took a few steps back towards my friends. I heard Benjamin scream out, "Are you okay? I'm coming up."

I went a bit farther down and yelled out, "Yeah, I'm coming down. Don't make any more noise."

Geoffrey quietly said, "The others are outside with Jayland."

Avant licked his lips. "Ah, the wolves. Are they still alive?"

I turned back to face him. "What did you do to them?"

He tapped his bony fingers along the stair-rail. "They're how you found us. They had to pay. My other question though…" He quickly stepped down the stairs and stood right in front of me, barely a foot between us. "…My other question though, how did you all break through my wards?"

C'mon Mason. Don't back down to him. I forced my body to stand its ground.

He let out his creepy laugh. "Oh, you're trying to be brave? My brother, it's okay to run back to your pathetic kin. I'd love to see him and his Fae…friend?"

He pushed my shoulder and I stepped back onto the fourth floor. Benjy and Geoffrey ran to my side. Geoffrey put his hand on my shoulder. "Mason, are you okay? Where's Avant?"

I pointed at the stairs as Avant walked down them. His evil grin sent chills down my spine. "Hello Benjamin. Hello, Fae." When he spit out the word 'Fae', I could feel his disgust.

Geoffrey stepped back as Benjamin shoved forward. "Avant, I see you're still Malute's little bellboy?"

The comment didn't even make him twitch. Benjy went on, "Why are you all hoarding the Shyne here? How come they are in such a dormant state?"

Avant looked over at the Shyne. He spoke now. "You all don't belong here. Malute will be very disappointed. Looks like I am going to have to get rid of you all by myself."

He raised his hands and I saw a violet orb building in his palm. I mumbled to Benjy. "Do you see that? How is he controlling an orb? I thought only Malute could do that."

Benjamin looked closer at Avant's hands. He whispered to Geoffrey, "Um, babe, do you see that?"

Geoffrey looked at us and then lifted his hands. A strong wind kicked up around us as Geoffrey started to manipulate the air in the room. Avant threw a violet orb towards us and laughed. "I wouldn't try to do anything brave, Fae."

We all flew back and looked up to make sure the Shyne weren't coming towards us. Shocked, I asked Benjamin, "How are they still not moving? How could they not have heard that?"

Avant threw another orb towards us and shouted out, "They will move when we need them to. You all will not ruin our plans. Get out!" He quickly tossed another orb towards us. We got up and started running down the stairs.

Mackenna and Layla were at the entrance of the first floor. Layla cried out, "Mason, they're dead! Royce and Marcus are dead!"

VIIII.

Trying to catch my breath, I ran over and hugged her.

"Tyler is outside with Jayland. He just called your Mimaw. She said Darcy's dad is on his way to Dallas now." Mackenna said softly.

Mackenna asked Geoffrey, "What happened up there?"

Geoffrey glanced at Benjy and then said, "Avant is here. He's gotten stronger. We need to get out of here, now!"

Ashton and Aden came into the building. Ashton sighed. "Hey y'all, Tyler and

Jayland just went back to y'alls apartment."

Aden added, "You all should go on to the apartment. We'll take care of the bodies."

I looked at Benjy and Geoffrey, then nodded. "Okay, sounds good."

Mackenna spoke up, "Are you all kidding me? Avant is here and we're running away? We need to kick his little ass and get him to tell us where Malute is."

Geoffrey's frustration showed through his eyes. "Mack, we've got to pick and choose our battles. This is not one that we want to pick, got it?"

She huffed. "No, I don't. Layla, don't you think we should go up there and show this creep a lesson?"

Layla looked at me for confirmation. "I think Geoffrey is right. We should go back to the apartment and regroup. We know where he is, we can always come back later."

Mackenna stared at us for a couple of seconds and then stomped off. "I'll be in the car; this is a joke."

We sat in the vehicle in silence when Layla finally talked. "So, what exactly happened upstairs? Why did you all come running down?"

I put my arm around her. "Avant was up there with a bunch of Shyne."

She gasped and scooted closer to me. "Are you serious? Did they attack y'all?"

I shook my head. Geoffrey answered, "No, the damn things were in some kind of a sedated state."

Benjamin went on, "I'm gonna need to call Maw about this when we get back. I've never heard of anything like this happening before."

Mackenna erupted, "If there were a lot of Shyne there, why didn't we torch the damn place?"

I looked at her, "Um, remember when Geoffrey said that Avant grew stronger? Well he was throwing damn orbs at us, just like Malute did."

Mackenna and Layla both covered their mouths, in shock. Layla asked, "How did he get that power all of a sudden?"

For a while no one said anything to that. Then Benjamin said, "I'm not sure, but it looks like Malute's been pretty busy in Dallas."

As Benjy finished saying that, Geoffrey's cell phone rang. He answered it on speaker phone, "Hello? Tyler? Is everything okay?"

Tyler quietly responded, "I-I don't know. Jayland and I got back to the apartment and he went crazy. He kind of…he kind of transformed in the living room."

Geoffrey and Benjamin mumbled together, "Crap".

Tyler went on, "I tried to calm him down but he just took off."

Benjy asked, "What do you mean he took off? He ran out of the apartment, fully transformed?"

Ty whispered, "Uh, yeah. I don't think anyone saw him, but I can't be totally sure. I listened through some of our neighbors' doors and I don't get the sense of anyone freaking out."

Geoffrey held his phone in his hand, "Tyler, wait there. We're down the street and will be there shortly."

When Ty and Geoffrey hung up, I asked, "What does Tyler mean Jayland transformed? I know he's a wolf, but there's no moon out. It's not even nighttime yet."

Benjamin looked at me through his rearview mirror. "Mason, the Smithwicks are true wolves. They're born into their powers, not bitten."

Geoffrey continued on from what Benjy had said, "Ah, young Sheer. You're strong, but you still have so much to learn."

X.

We pulled into the apartment complex and all ran into Jayland's apartment.

What the hell happened here? That was my first thought. The kitchen table's glass was completely shattered. The television was broken in pieces all over the living room and the leather sofas were completely ripped up.

Geoffrey quietly picked up some of the bigger pieces of glass as Benjamin asked. "Tyler, what exactly set him off? Are you okay? Did he try to hurt you?"

Tyler looked at us, with horror in his eyes. "I'm okay. I don't know what really pushed him over the edge, but when he came in here he just started crying. He was crying and shaking. I tried to talk to him but he told me to get away from him. I went to the bathroom and when I came back out he was transforming into his wolf form."

Mackenna hugged Tyler as Benjamin pulled out his cell phone. "Mason, I'm going to call Mimaw. I am sure she's going to flip out when she hears about Jayland going outside fully transformed."

I nodded and started to pick up pieces of the sofa. Layla to help Geoffrey with the glass. She asked, "Do you think Mr. Smithwick is coming because of Marcus and Royce's deaths or because Jayland has gone crazy?"

Mackenna snorted, "Damn, cuz. You make me proud, I knew you had a little bitch in you."

Geoffrey looked up and glared at Mack. He continued to pick up the glass and asked, "So is anyone else freaking out that an angry, grieving werewolf is running around Dallas?"

I mumbled, "Let's just hope we can find him before he hurts anyone. The last thing we need is for him to go AWOL on us."

We all stayed quiet for a bit, cleaning up Jayland's mess until Ashton and Aden walked into the apartment. Aden huffed, "Oh, um, wow. Is everyone okay?"

Tyler answered before Mackenna could, "Yeah, we're all fine. The sofa and table however, are definitely not."

Ashton started to help us clean the mess when Benjy asked him, "What did you all do with the Smithwicks' bodies?"

Aden joined in on the cleaning and answered Benjamin for his brother. "We took the bodies to our council's church. They're taking care of them until someone can go and give them a proper burial."

Mackenna sat on the floor, against the torn-up sofa. "So, any idea as to what we should do, now that you all let Avant and those things get away?"

Geoffrey let out a huffing sound. "Don't be so dramatic, Mackenna. We let him go for a good reason. If we'd stayed, I doubt any of us would have made it out alive. There were far too many of those Shyne."

I leaned on what was left of the sofa and took a long, deep breath. "Geoffrey's right. If we had stayed, Avant probably would have woken up the Shyne. I'm not sure that we would have been able to take on a hundred of them on our own."

Benjamin came over to me and took a seat on the floor across from me. "Cuz, I think that we did the right thing by leaving, but I'm sure you would have known exactly what to do with the Shyne. You're a lot stronger than you're giving yourself credit for."

Layla quit cleaning and chimed in. "He's right, Mason. You're getting stronger every day. Have you talked to Mimaw about your powers yet? Does she know that you're able to communicate with your ancestors so easily?"

I shook my head. Just then the front door flew open. Jayland was standing at the front door wearing only his boxer shorts. His chiseled abs were glistening with sweat and Geoffrey took in a deep breath. "Jayland, you're offering a very nice sight for us all but may I suggest you get some clothes on now that your tantrum has settled?"

I noticed he had dried blood on his neck as he closed the apartment door. He said nothing. Mackenna asked, "Did you hurt someone on your little rampage or did you just go hunting for a bunny?"

Jayland's eyes were as dark as night and he mumbled, "Do not joke with me, Wrightpress."

Tyler gave Mackenna an ugly stare-down. He walked towards Jayland and put his hand on his shoulder. "Are you alright, dude? You had us all worried."

Jayland's jaw stayed tight as he silently nodded. Then he sighed, "I called Darcy's dad. He's not coming after all. I want to be the one to track down and kill those bastards. And from what they've told me, Casey Adams has demanded she come to Dallas to help."

Mackenna protested, "Her? You've got to be kidding me. There's no way in hell we can work together!"

He looked at her and then at the rest of us. "I know it'll probably be a little bit challenging but I think she'd be more helpful to me than my relatives at this point. I am going to ask that you put your differences aside for the sake of my sanity."

We all stayed quiet and looked at each other. He continued, "So, are you all going to help me or not?"

We all stood up and went in to hug Jayland as he pushed us back and let out his creepy laugh. "Okay, don't come any closer. I probably stink and I'm in boxers, for God's sake."

XI.

A few days later Mimaw called me, waking me up in the middle of the night. "Mason, Mason baby, you all need to get up, now!"

I squinted my eyes and looked at the time that was glowing brightly on my alarm clock. "Maw? What's going on? It's four in the morning."

Maw's cry came through the phone and I jumped up. "Maw, what's going on? Are you okay?"

"Mason, are you near a TV? Turn it on to the news, boy."

I reached over to my antique nightstand and grabbed the remote to my smart TV. I turned it on and flipped it to the local news station. I dropped the phone and yelled out, "Benjy! Geoffrey! Get up! Come here, hurry!"

A second later the guys were in my room, in matching bathrobes. Benjy asked, "What is it Mason? Is Mimaw okay?"

Crap, Mimaw. I leaned down to pick the phone back up. "Maw, I just woke Benjy up. We're going to get everyone together now. I'll call you once we have come up with a plan."

"Okay, you boys be safe. I-I love you all."

I hung up the phone and looked at my cousin who was hugging his boyfriend tightly. Geoffrey shouted, "Mackenna, Layla, get in here!"

We all sat down on my bed and stared at the television until the girls came into the room. Layla let out a long yawn as Mackenna came in, grunting.

I pointed at the screen and saw them both snap out of their exhaustion immediately. Layla asked, "Did this just happen? Are they here in Dallas?"

Benjy shrugged and put his finger on his mouth to silence us all. The news reporter started to speak, "…We are reporting live from midtown Dallas this morning. There have been numerous earthquakes reported and as you can see, buildings have collapsed into the ground. Emergency responders are on the scene and we will keep you updated as we get more information."

As the reporter sent the broadcast back to scheduled programming, a scroll on the bottom of the screen showed that a projected number of around 170 people had been reported as missing or were unaccounted for.

Layla and Mackenna looked at us. Mack got her cell phone out and called Tyler. "Tyler, you all need to come to the apartment. Yes, right now!"

Layla had tears falling from her eyes. "Do you think they're bringing more Shyne into Dallas? Where did all those people go?"

Benjy responded, "I think that Malute made a little deal with someone powerful on the other side. Human souls doomed to Sinara, in exchange for more Shyne."

I got up to hug Layla and felt a tug in my chest. I grabbed my t-shirt in pain. I looked around at my friends, in a panic. "Malute's trying to communicate with me. Get everyone here now."

I fell into the now-familiar darkness and heard the loud **BANG! BANG!** Malute's deep voice soon followed. "Mason, my son, Avant told me that you two had an unexpected and unwanted meeting. He also tells me that he had to relocate all of my Shyne because of your foolish friends. How dare you go into one of my homes, uninvited."

"You did a pretty good job trying to keep us out. Sadly for you, it looks like your wards were not strong enough to keep us out. More specifically, to keep me out. Why did you hurt the mundanes? I know it was you, so don't try to deny it."

"Do not ask me questions when you already know the answers. May I ask though, why are you so concerned about the mundanes? They are here for our taking. They are at the very bottom of the food chain. They are disposable."

I shouted, "They are not disposable! They are here for a reason. They can express things that you are not capable of. Like love and compassion!"

"Be warned, my son, if you continue to get in my way I will dispose of your pathetic loved ones."

I was thrown back into reality and saw that everyone, including the Hood brothers and Tyler were standing around me. Benjy asked, "Was it Malute? Did he come to you? What did he say?"

Mackenna huffed, "For God's sake Benjamin, give him a second."

I let out a long sigh. "Yeah, it was him. He's pretty pissed that we found the Shyne." I looked at the Hood brothers. "Avant moved all of the Shyne. I'm not sure where, but they're not at the warehouse anymore."

Jayland protested, "Well that's just great! How are we going to find them now? Do you all realize how long it took us to find them in the first place?"

Everyone stayed quiet until Jayland's phone rang. He answered it, annoyed, "Hello?"

He mumbled for a couple of minutes and then hung up. He put the phone in his back pocket. "Casey's here. Mackenna, would you like to help her with her things?"

Layla laughed as her cousin showed a disgusted expression. Jayland grinned mischievously. "I guess I'll go get her then. Anyone else care to help?"

Mackenna gave Tyler a warning look and then Geoffrey spoke. "Good lord, I'll help you. Let's get a move on, we have lots to do today."

XII.

A few hours later, we finished breakfast and got Casey all caught up. She was waiting for us by the front door when she spoke. "Does anyone here care about how this place looks? No matching furniture. No matching silverware. What is really going on here?"

She looked at Mackenna and added, "I expected so much more from you Wrightpress girls."

Mackenna made a noise like a growl as Layla laughed it off. "We just thought we'd leave the decorating to someone a bit more shallow. I'm really glad you're here now."

Geoffrey and Benjamin came into the living room with belts that held a bunch of different weapons. Tyler asked, "Are those tool-belts really necessary? I mean, do you think that a taser is going to take Avant down?"

We all giggled but Geoffrey looked highly annoyed. "Are you kids done with your bullying?"

We all looked down, embarrassed, as he went on. "Benjamin and I have come up with a plan and we think we know where Avant may have moved the Shyne."

"Where do you think they're at? Do you think they're still in Dallas?" I asked.

"Mason, I think Avant took them to your old neighborhood. There aren't any mundanes there and it's kind of fitting, don't you think?" Benjy replied.

Layla grabbed my hand and squeezed it tightly. "Are you going to be okay if we go back?"

"Why would he take them back to your old neighborhood? Are we missing something?" Ashton asked.

Tyler explained what happened there while Layla and I went outside. I put my arms around her as we leaned on the rail of the balcony that looked over the apartment complex's parking area. We stood in silence for a couple of minutes then she asked, "So, you never answered me."

I raised my eyebrow. "What do you mean?"

She pulled out of my embrace and looked into my eyes. "Are you going to be okay if we go back to where your mother was killed? Where you found out Malute was your dad?"

I shrugged. "I really don't know. I don't know if the Shyne will be there, but maybe it is the right thing for us to do. Maybe we can get some clue as to what happened there. I need to know what exactly happened to my mom. How can Malute be my dad?"

She put her hand on my face and looked at me with a worried expression. "I just don't want you to get hurt. I lost my dad and I don't know what I'd do without you."

I tried to shrug off my nerves and reassured her. "I'll be okay. I just need to find out what really happened. If I can find out that, I think it'll help us kill Malute for good."

As I finished speaking, the gang came out of the apartment. Tyler let out a long sigh. "Alright, everyone is caught up and ready to go. Mase, you down to go back there?"

I nodded and then started to walk down to the vehicle.

XIII.

As we got closer to the place I visit in my nightmare every night, I started to feel dizzy. Layla must have noticed because she quickly started to rub her hand on mine.

She whispered, "Just take long, deep breaths. You'll be okay."

I squeezed her hand and took her advice. Mackenna spoke up, "Um, Mason, don't barf in here. I will literally kill you."

Tyler laughed, "Calm down, babe. He's not going to puke."

Casey joined in. "Um, I'm not too sure about that. Look at him."

Benjamin looked at me in his mirror and asked, "Mason, are you sure you're okay? If you can't do this, you can take the other car and head back to the apartment."

"Um, yeah. I'll be fine. Park in the driveway and just give me a second."

Benjamin parked the SUV in the driveway of my dreaded home and everyone stepped out to give me a minute to myself.

I closed my eyes and reached out to my ancestors on the other side. "Fitzgerald Sheers, please help me through this. Help me find what I came for."

The now-familiar voice answered me. "My child, we are here with you. You are doing the right thing."

I asked her, "Are the Shyne here?"

"I am not sure. We are unable to track them."

I let out a frustrated sigh as my relative interrupted. "Do not worry, young Sheer. I repeat, you are doing the right thing. The answer to your parent's death is most definitely here."

"What happened to my mom? We all know my *dad* survived."

Instead of answering the question about my mom, she questioned me, "Are you sure your father survived? Don't let Malute fool you. He is a body jumper. His evil soul has taken over your dad's body and it seems that it's only a temporary place for him. The power Malute holds has made his appearance unrecognizable. I promise you, your father was a good Sheer and a good man. The thing that is Malute is not that of the original Sheer."

I was about to ask what she meant by that when Mackenna's tapping on the window disturbed my concentration with the other side. Annoyed, I got out of the vehicle and slammed the door.

Mackenna stepped back, with her hands up to show surrender. "Slow down, dude. No need to be so angry. I was just hurrying you up a bit. I mean, we are a little cold out here."

Instead of responding, I walked past her and spoke to everyone. "Let's get in the house. I think it's the best place for us to start."

XIV.

As we walked from the driveway towards the house, I started to feel faint. I felt a stabbing pain in my stomach as I leaned over and threw up. Layla rubbed my back and she handed me a bottle of water. "Are you okay? You don't have to go in, if you don't want to. I can stay with you here, while everyone goes in and starts to look around."

I shook my head as I gargled some water and then spit it out. "I have to go in there. It's the only way I'll get any clue as to what we need to do."

Benjy forced the front door open and we all went into the house. The familiar foul odor of the place hit me and everyone started to gag as I walked towards the closet I've grown familiar with in my dreams. I peeked inside and took a deep breath as I heard Mackenna complaining about the smell.

I let out a long sigh and right before I closed the closet door I noticed a small floorboard was lifted towards the back of the closet. I knelt down on my knees and dusted off the floor. I leaned into the closet and started to lift the board. I pulled it up easily and then it made a loud cracking sound and snapped in half.

I looked behind me and noticed that Geoffrey and Layla were standing there. Geoffrey's eyes lit up as he asked, "What did you find? How did you know to come in here?"

"This is where I hide in my nightmare. I'm always hiding here with the younger version of myself."

I turned back around and put my hand into the floor. I felt a big book and tried to pull it out from the floor.

Layla asked, "What is it?"

I was struggling to get the book through the small gap and muttered, "I think it's a book. It's too big for this hole though. I need to pull up another floorboard."

Tyler walked over and cleared his throat. "Want a real man to pull the board up?"

I showed off my favorite hand gesture to him and got up so he could fit into the closet. He pulled up three boards with little effort. He dusted off a black book and turned around with a smile across his face.

Annoyed, I grabbed the book from him. The second I touched the book a warm, silver liquid poured from my palm into the spine of it. The book's lock opened and the title of the book,*Fitzgerald*, showed in bright yellow.

Layla asked, "I thought your Mimaw had your family's Brasta?"

I shrugged. "I thought so, too."

"Benjamin, can you come in here please," Geoffrey shouted out.

My cousin was with us in a matter of seconds. His mouth dropped. "Mason, where did you find that?"

I pointed at the broken floor in the closet. I asked, "What is it?"

He swallowed. "It is the original Sheer Brasta. It has always been rumored that it was destroyed years ago. I don't understand."

Before he could continue explaining, we heard the train-like bang sound off from outside of the house. We all looked at each other in a panic as Ashton ran towards us. "There was a bright flash of light in the forest. I think Avant is here!"

I got the Brasta, tucked it into my jeans and turned to face my friends. "We need to go out there and find him."

Jayland and Casey were the first out of the house. They started to run and slowly, their bodies started to transform. Jayland let out a cry that quickly turned into a howl as he headed into the forest. His fur was as black as night with grey spots around his eyes.

Casey ran a few steps behind him and as she transformed into her wolf, I noticed that her fur was a light brown. Tyler mumbled, "Do you think Casey would dye her fur if she could?"

I let out a small laugh as I followed my friends into the forest.

XV.

We entered the dark forest and my insides immediately froze. A chill went from my stomach through my spine and then suddenly, it was in my neck. Layla grabbed my hand. "Take your time. You can do this, we're all here for you."

Tyler zoomed past Layla and I and then shouted out, "Dude, c'mon, you all are walking way too slow!"

I smiled and yelled back, "Not all of us have that weird vamp speed."

Mackenna came up to us, grunting. "Don't flatter him. If his head gets any bigger, it might just explode."

Tyler's facial expression went grim. "No need for all of y'alls negativity."

Benjy, Ashton, Aden and Geoffrey joined us and were all smiles as they caught the conversation exchange. Geoffrey was about to start talking when we heard loud howls from the forest up ahead.

We ran to join Tyler and then proceeded to move towards the dog-like sounds that we continued to hear from deep in the forest.

A few minutes later, we were all standing beside Jayland and Casey, who were back in their human bodies.

Aden asked, "What happened? Why were you all howling?"

Casey was still trying to get her clothes back on while Jayland responded. "We picked up on the Shyne's scent. They're here, somewhere close by."

Casey huffed, "They smell like rotting sewage. It is disgusting. Don't y'all smell it?"

Tyler nodded but the rest of us shook our heads. Mackenna took a deep breath. "I don't smell anything."

Benjamin spoke, "None of us are likely to be able to. Tyler, Jayland and Casey have extraordinary smelling senses. We, however, haven't been blessed with that."

Tyler smiled. "Oh, yeah. They smell like death. Macky, babe, be happy you can't smell it."

Mackenna's lips tightened as the loud bang sounded off a couple of hundred feet from where we were standing. We all looked at each other and then ran towards the sound.

The Wrightpresses were in full Fae mode as they were all already starting to access their elements. Casey and Jayland stayed in human form but they had their sharp werewolf teeth gleaming through their mouths. Tyler's eyes had a tint to them and his fangs were fully out.

The Hood brothers, Benjy and I were all ready to start putting up wards when Avant's low, groaning laugh broke our concentration.

"Why are you so persistent on becoming my enemy, Mason? I am not someone you want to cross swords with. Father would be very disappointed in you."

I spit at the ground, my hands were now shaking. "I'm not trying to become your friend or your enemy. I'm trying to kill you."

"You're an idiot! You know that I cannot die! It is not possible. Malute has made us immortal."

The Wrightpresses kicked up a strong wind, which accompanied a heavy rainfall. Mackenna winked at me and then jumped up and threw a ball of fire in Avant's direction.

Benjy whispered, "She's not trying to hit him with the fire. They're distracting him."

Avant grinned, showing off his sharp, rotting teeth. "You Fae don't give up, do you?"

Mackenna snorted and then did a back flip as a lightning bolt hit the ground right behind Avant. In the brilliance of the lightning, we saw the Shyne hiding near the trees behind him.

Avant lifted his hands and a dark orb started to form in his hands. "I'm going to get rid of you all, once and for all. I am sick of you Fae!"

Avant was about to release the orb when Casey and Jayland bit into his shoulders and held him down. Tyler ran from behind them and then took a bite out of Avant's neck.

A thick, black, oily substance started spouting from Avant's neck as he screamed out in pain. "What have you done? What do you think you're doing?"

Benjamin started to walk towards Avant. "My cousin told you what we are here to do. We are here to kill you."

Geoffrey, Mackenna and Layla stood behind the Hood brothers. Ashton spoke now. "You say that you cannot die, but you are most definitely wrong."

Casey and Jayland were holding down Avant as Tyler leaned over and spit out the oil-like blood and started to gag. Mackenna yelled out, "Ty, are you alright?"

He held up his hand and continued to throw up. "Yeah, I think. His blood, it's not really blood. It tastes like I just drank out of a garbage disposal."

Mackenna made a disgusted face as she walked towards him with a bottle of water. Avant's eyes looked frightened now. He stuttered, "D-Do you all think I can actually die?"

He let out a nervous laugh and continued his train of thought. "Malute will never let that happen! I am too valuable."

The second he finished his sentence, a loud train-like noise blared off a few feet behind him and then, out of nothing, a thin woman appeared.

The thin lady was wearing a black robe and the hood covered her face in the darkness of the night. The only thing visible on her slim body was her glowing red eyes. She cleared her throat before speaking in an almost purring like voice. "Hello, Avant."

XVI.

Avant fell down to his knees and held tight onto his neck, trying to stop the oil-like blood from spewing out. The mysterious lady walked closer to Avant, paying us no attention. Mackenna whispered, "Who the hell is that?"

No one answered her as the hooded lady spoke again. "Avant, your father is very disappointed in you. You have failed him not once, but twice."

She walked around him in a circle. "He's so disappointed in you, that he called me back from New York for this. You know that this puts our plan way behind schedule, don't you? Tsk, tsk, what shall we do with you?"

Avant stuttered in a low, worried voice. "Ser-Seraphina, why did you come back? Why did Father call you here?"

She pointed at us, displaying a long bony finger. Her nails were razor sharp. She continued to walk around Avant as she pulled her hood back from her face. Her eyes seemed to glow brighter as she revealed her long, wavy red hair.

"Avant, you can no longer be trusted. For God's sake, look at you. You are struggling to fight with these—"

She paused and glanced at us for the first time since she materialized in front of us. Seraphina made eye contact with me and my insides froze.

She continued to talk to Avant, keeping her red eyes on me. "You are struggling to fight off these children. How can you expect us to trust you with more responsibility? You had to watch over the inactive Shyne and you could not even do that!"

Avant got back on his feet. "That is not my fault! The Sheers have wolves, Fae, and a vampire on their side! How am I supposed to keep the Shyne hidden from all of them? The wolves alone can find us easily, you know that."

Seraphina took her glare off me and then turned her furious gaze towards Avant. "Enough with your excuses! I've got wolves all over New York and I've kept our little secrets hidden just fine."

Avant rebutted, "You were a Fae! That should be easy for you to do. I don't have those abilities, remember?"

She stood in front of him now. She snapped her fingers and a small flame appeared in her palm. "I do remember my Fae ancestry, it's a good thing you do too."

Layla whispered. "She's a Fae?"

Geoffrey shrugged as I interrupted their exchange. "Who the hell are you? Why are you here?"

Seraphina turned her evil stare at me. "With that short temper and attitude, you must be Mason. It's a pleasure to finally meet you. I'm Seraphina and I'm your father's, um, well just call me his business partner."

I glared at her. "Malute is not my father! My father died when I was a kid."

She laughed as she turned back to face Avant. "Since you all are dying to know why I'm here, I guess I'll just spill the beans."

She put her long fingers on Avant's shoulder as she whispered to him, "I'm here to kill you."

XVII.

Avant's face went pale and he fell back down to his knees. He begged, "Seraphina, please don't do it! Give me another chance, please! I will not let you or Father down!"

She forcefully removed his hand from his throat, allowing the thick blood to drip out again. "You have already let him down, dear. And because I'm here and not in New York, you've let me down. You know how I feel about failure."

Avant's eyes were dimmed with worry as he continued to beg. "Can you just take me to Malute? Give me the chance to explain myself to him."

"You know that is not possible, Avant."

Seraphina stared down at her long nails and dusted them off with her other hand. "It's a shame, really. I just got these done."

She lifted her index finger and then wistfully dragged it across Avant's neck. The black oily blood started pouring out of his neck like a flood and his eyes widened in horror.

Seraphina looked back at us and then snapped her fingers. She was holding a bright flame as she said, "Mason, the next time we see each other, I hope you have ditched your loser friends and the attitude."

She turned back around and threw the flame onto Avant who was now rolling around the ground. We all looked at him, shocked, and covered our noses from the hideous smell as we heard the loud bang. Seraphina dematerialized behind Avant's now dead body. The flames were still burning his body as Geoffrey asked Benjamin, "Do you think we should put the fire out?"

Benjy looked at me; I gave him a nodded confirmation. Layla closed her eyes and lifted her hands to the sky. Almost immediately, a downpour of rain started and the fire that was consuming Avant's body was slowly extinguished.

Layla put her hands down when the fire was completely out and we all ran to assess what was left of his body. The smell was similar to a landfill site and his body was burnt to a crisp.

Mackenna huffed in disgust. "Dude, he reeks."

Ashton and Aden joined the rest of us as Casey asked, "So what exactly just happened here?"

I shrugged and Benjy answered for me. "Well, looks like Avant's dead, but who was that Seraphina lady?"

"I've heard of her before but I didn't think she'd ever be working with Malute. She's a Fae who is into some pretty dark stuff back home. I've heard her name come up a few times but I just thought she was another rogue Fae," Jayland said.

"Do you think you can reach out to some of your contacts in New York to see what they know about her? I find it quite troubling that she said she's business partners with Malute," Benjamin said.

"Do you think that Malute really wanted Avant dead? Didn't he consider Avant as his son?" Ashton asked.

Aden continued his brother's train of thought, "What do you all think that Seraphina is doing here?"

Jayland replied, "I'll reach out to some people back home. And I don't know what Seraphina has planned, but whatever it is, it can't be good."

XVIII.

We all headed back to the apartment. Layla sat next to me in the car as Benjy and Geoffrey sat in the front seat. Layla cuddled close to me. "What are you thinking about?"

I leaned my head on hers and then sighed before answering her. "I don't know. I guess I'm kind of bummed about not being able to get some answers out of Avant before he died."

Layla squeezed my hand with hers and I continued. "And I'm thinking about Seraphina. Did you see the way she looked at me? When she looked at me it was like she was looking inside of me. As if she looked at my soul. It's weird, I know, but my insides completely froze."

She looked up at me, worry in her eyes. "I know they said she was a Fae, but I think it's a little strange that she was able to dematerialize like Malute. Don't you?"

Geoffrey answered her from his place in the front. "That Seraphina was something else, huh? Red hair, red eyes? That's a little more than weird. She obviously has Fae powers, but I've never seen a Fae that looks like her."

Benjy added, "Yeah, I have never even heard about a Fae with powers or looks like hers. It's a little odd."

My cousin looked at me through the rearview mirror. "I think we're going to need to have a little chat with Maw. Maybe she'll know something about Seraphina."

I nodded. "Yeah, I'll give her a call as soon as we get back to the apartment."

I looked at Layla and she gave me a reassuring smile. "Is it weird that I'm kind of bummed Avant's dead, too? I know Mack and I really wanted to mess with him a bit before you all had to—you know—kill him."

"Yeah, I think Mackenna would've loved to torture him. A lot. She'll use that little flame of hers whenever she can, huh?"

"Yeah, she definitely will."

We finally pulled up to our apartment complex and we all headed up to get some food. My friends went into the apartment while I stuck around outside so I could call Mimaw in private.

Tyler looked at me before he walked inside. "You alright, man?"

I nodded and then went inside. I pulled my cell phone out and called Maw. She answered almost immediately. "Mason, everything alright baby? What's going on?"

I looked at the phone and noticed it was well past midnight. "Maw, I'm sorry I didn't think to check the time before I called you. Yeah, everything is okay. Something kind of strange happened tonight."

Maw let out a long sigh. "Don't you worry about waking me up. What is it? What happened tonight?"

I sat down on the sidewalk and started to tell Maw how we went to the house in my nightmare. "Maw, when I went into the closet, I found a book. It had our last name in bright yellow letters on the cover."

Mimaw let out what sounded like a low cry. "My God, Mason. Were you able to open it?"

I stayed quiet for a second and then stood up to get the book out of my jeans. She pushed on, "Mason, I asked you something, boy."

I sat back down and put the book on my lap. I stuttered, "Ye-yes ma'am. Not at first though. The silver mist from my hands actually opened the book."

"Mason, what else happened?"

I told her what happened earlier in the night and when I got to the part about Seraphina appearing, Maw gasped. "Are you sure she said her name was Seraphina? What did she look like?"

I scratched my head and remembered her bright, red hair and eyes. "Um, she had really red hair. And her eyes were kinda red, too."

Mimaw stayed quiet for a couple of seconds and then I heard some papers shuffling around. "Maw, what are you doing?"

She shushed me and then asked, "Mason, you and Benjy need to go through the book you found. You two need to figure out how it found you. I'd start first thing in the morning if I were you."

I asked, "Is this our family's Brasta? I thought you had the Fitzgerald Brasta?"

She gave me a hesitant answer. "It sounds like you found the original Fitzgerald Brasta. That Brasta was supposed to have been burned with the first Fitzgerald Sheer."

I looked at the book and felt the warm, tingly sensation in my palms. "So, if this Brasta was burned with the original Fitzgerald Sheer, how am I holding it? How was it under the floorboards of that house?"

Maw almost shouted at me. "I don't know Mason! I just don't know. I'm going to be up all night doing some research and talking with our family on the other side. Like I said, you get some sleep and then go through the Brasta with Benjy in the morning. I'll call you if I find out anything."

I stood up. "Alright, Maw. Good night. I love you."

XIX.

The next morning Benjy and I headed out for a run while everyone started getting ready for what was definitely going to be a long day. As my cousin and I finished the last leg of our run I asked, "How do you think the original Brasta showed up in that house last night?"

He looked over at me and took a drink of his water. "I don't know. I've been thinking about that all night."

Benjy slowed his run to a jog and then continued, "I was talking to Geoffrey about it in bed last night. It's kind of weird that the original Fitzgerald Brasta just randomly showed up on the exact same night that Seraphina showed up.

And on the same night that Seraphina just happened to be sent to kill Avant."

I matched my cousin's slowing pace and tried to catch my breath. "Yeah, that is all a little weird. I called Mimaw when we got to the apartment last night."

"Was she pissed that you woke her up?"

"Nah. She was actually a little worried when she answered. It's like she knew I was going to call."

"Well, she probably had one of her infamous feelings. You know she is strangely intuitive."

I slowed down my jog and wiped the sweat from my brows. "Everything about last night seems off. When Seraphina showed up and looked at me, I just had this strange feeling. I feel like I've seen her before, maybe. I don't know. She just stared into like, my soul. I know they said she was a Fae but how is she a Fae and yet like Malute? How is she not just another Shyne?"

Benjy tried to control his breathing. "Yeah, she's definitely different. She was able to dematerialize and that's weird in itself. There's not much known about how certain beings are able to dematerialize. I'm afraid there are a lot more creatures in this world than we know."

I looked at him, puzzled. "You're saying that you think there are more than Sheers, vampires, werewolves, Fae and Shyne? Why am I not surprised?"

He laughed. "Yeah, that's exactly what I'm saying. Just a few months ago you thought there were only mundanes, right? Who's to say that there aren't more beings in this world that we haven't come across? The world is an old and strange place, Mason."

I nodded in agreement. "Yeah, I guess you're right."

As I finished speaking, my cell phone rang. I looked at the screen and saw that it was an anonymous facetime call. I stared at my cousin, who was already leaning in and looking to see who it was.

He asked, "An anonymous call? At 8am?"

I shrugged my shoulders and picked up the call. Seraphina appeared on the screen after a couple of seconds. "Hello, Mason. I hope you slept well."

I felt my heart start to race. "What do you want? How did you get my number?" I demanded.

Her red eyes glowed brightly through the screen. "I have my ways, sweet-stuff."

She started to play with her bright red-orange hair. "I wanted to see if you were able to meet me for lunch today. I feel like there is a lot for us to talk about."

"Why would we have anything to talk about? If you're working with Malute like you say you are, you know that he and I don't exactly see eye to eye."

She continued to play with her hair in a flirtatious way. "Aw, sweet-stuff. Don't worry about my business with Malute. Business is business. We, however, have a lot of personal things we can and need to talk about."

I looked over at Benjy as Seraphina let out a long huff. "Sweet-stuff, don't be rude. Do we have a lunch date or not?"

I glared at her through the cell phone. "Yeah, I can do that. Where do you want to meet?"

She was now beaming in triumph. "I know this little diner on Highway 45. Meet me there at 2pm."

I was about to end the call when she added, "Oh and come alone. I'll know if you don't."

She ended the call and Benjy hit me. "Why would you agree to meet with her? She's working with Malute, Mason. Do you think it's actually a good idea to go somewhere with her? And alone for that matter? I'm going to call Maw."

He pulled out his cell phone and I instantly snatched it from him. "Dude, don't call Mimaw. She'll just freak out. I'm going to be fine. I can handle myself."

He looked at me, annoyed. "Are you sure about that? Every time we've been faced with some kind of challenge, you either black out, faint or get sick. Do you think you can really handle yourself?"

"Shut up. You know I only feel that way when Malute is around. And it's because he's trying to control my mind, remember?"

My cousin snatched his phone back from me and put it in his pocket. "Let's go back to the apartment and tell everyone about the little meeting you've set up, see what they all have to say about it."

XX.

We drove back to the apartment in an awkward silence and when we pulled into our parking lot, Geoffrey, Mackenna and Layla were standing outside.

Layla jogged over to the car with a smile spread across her perfect face. "Hey babe, how was your run this morning?"

I hugged her and then stepped back. "Hey, uh, it was pretty good."

She looked at me with a puzzled face. "Are you alright?"

Benjamin walked up and cleared his throat. "Tell her Mason, tell her and everyone else what you've done."

I rolled my eyes in defeat as Geoffrey and Mackenna came over. Geoffrey hugged Benjamin and leaned in for a kiss. "Hey there, my sexy man."

The tension was heavy as my cousin coldly reciprocated the kiss. Mackenna asked, "What's going on?"

Layla put her cold hand on my arm. "What's he talking about? What did you do?"

I moved my arm away from Layla and took a deep breath. "When we were finishing our run, I got a facetime call from Seraphina."

Layla's eyes narrowed as she asked, "Okay and then what?"

I continued, "She asked me to meet her for lunch this afternoon. She said that we have a lot that we need to talk about."

Mackenna groaned, "How did that red-headed psychopath get your phone number?"

Geoffrey asked, "Better yet, what does she want to meet with you about?"

I looked at them all, trying to hold back the annoyance in my voice. "I don't know how she got my number, and I don't know exactly what she wants to meet about."

Layla declared, "Okay, so then we'll all go with you."

I shook my head. "No, she said that I needed to go alone. And that she'd know if anyone went with me."

Mackenna spoke out, "You have got to be kidding me. You did hear her say that she's working with Malute, right? You did see what she was able to do to Avant, right?"

I stayed quiet but shook my head. Layla quietly asked, "And you're still going with her?"

I nodded. "I have to. I need to know what she's got planned. Or why she's even working with Malute."

Everyone stayed quiet for a couple of seconds and then Benjamin said, "Mason, I think that you are an idiot for agreeing to meet with her. But, I do think that there's a way you can have back up without us being there."

I looked at him, confused. He continued, "The ancestors on the other side. Why don't you call upon them and let them know what you're doing. I'm sure that they can help protect you."

I let out a sigh of relief. "I don't know why I didn't think about that. That's perfect, Benjy!"

Layla kept her attention on me; that she was still annoyed showed in her eyes. "So, what are we all supposed to do while you're meeting with this deadly Fae-thing?"

My cousin answered for me. "We can all be on alert close by, but far enough to satisfy Seraphina's request."

Geoffrey hugged Benjamin again. "And this, my dear, is why I love you."

Mackenna let out a sound that was similar to a growl. "So are we seriously going to let Mason meet up with that psycho? Who's to say she isn't going to just burn him to ashes?"

Benjamin answered, "We don't know that she won't. All we can do is hope, I guess."

XXI.

As I finished getting ready I sat on my bed to clear my mind. I closed my eyes and my ancestor's familiar voice came booming through.

"Mason, do not trust Seraphina. She is a powerful creature. She is someone, or rather something, that you do not want to get involved with."

"I know, but I have to meet her. I need to know why she killed Avant. I need to know why she's working with Malute."

"Do not try to trick her. She will know that your friends are close by. She is no fool."

I let out a long sigh. "So what should I do? You said it yourself, I can't trust her."

My ancestor's voice grew louder. "Do not mock me, boy. You need to go alone. We are here to help you from the other side. We will shield you and she will be unable to detect us."

I nodded my head as if she could see me and let out a quiet laugh. I opened my eyes and looked over at the shut door. I could hear my friends talking about what was about to happen. I closed my eyes again and mumbled, "I need to tell them the plan. I need them to know that I'm going alone but that you all will be here there with me. I don't want them to try and be superheroes and get themselves hurt."

The voice in my head shouted, "Do not tell them that we will be there with you. You need to just demand that they not go.

They need to stay here, for their safety and yours."

"How the hell am I going to convince them to let me go alone? That's just not going to happen. Have you seen who my friends are? They're a bit of a demanding bunch."

Before the lady in my head could respond, Layla and Benjamin walked into the room. Layla asked, "Who were you talking to? What's going on?"

Benjy took a closer look at me. "You were talking to the ancestors, weren't you? What did they say? What are they telling you to do? Do they know who Seraphina is?"

I stood up, trying to hide my annoyance. "Yes I was talking to them and they want me to go alone and—"

The pair of them interrupted me, "—
They're crazy!"

"I have to go alone and that's that. You all
need to stay here. Benjamin, why don't
you try to go through the Brasta and read
up on Seraphina. Maybe you can find
something that's related to her. We need
to find out what she is."

Tyler walked in the room. "Hey guys,
Ashton and Aden just went home for the
day. They had some stuff they had to take
care of. They want me to let them know
what happens when we get back."

He looked at me and then at Layla and
my cousin. "We're not going with you
anymore, are we?"

Layla folded her arms and answered.
"No, we're not. Mason is listening to his
crazy ancestors that are dead in some
spirit world."

She glared at me as Tyler hit me on the arm. "Dude, you have got to be kidding me. We're not going with you because your dead ancestors told you we can't? Who's going to help protect you if Seraphina decides to go batshit crazy again?"

Mackenna and Geoffrey joined us in the small room and Geoffrey added, "Hell, who's going to help protect you if Malute shows up? What if it's all just a set-up?"

Layla kept her arms tightly folded. "Apparently Mason has it all covered. The people on the other side have it all figured out and they'll help him." She glared at me and then spoke to Mackenna and Geoffrey, "Do y'all want to go to a movie? I'm over this."

Mackenna looked impressed with her cousin. "Yeah, let's go do that."

She leaned in to give Tyler a kiss as Casey and Jayland came into the overly crowded bedroom. "I'll call you when the movie is over. We can have dinner or something."

Tyler blushed "Alright, sounds good babe. See ya'"

Geoffrey kissed Benjy goodbye as Layla stomped out of the room without saying a word to me. I threw a pillow across the room. Geoffrey mumbled, "Good luck with this one. Looks like there's a little bit of trouble in paradise. Call me if you need something."

Benjy walked Geoffrey and the girls outside while Tyler stayed behind with Casey and Jayland. Jayland asked, "You're not really going alone, right? Please tell me it was just a ploy to keep the Fae safe."

I shook my head and grabbed the car keys. "Nah, I have to go alone. I'm going to be fine. I just need to get us some answers."

Casey asked, "I don't want to be melodramatic like the Wrightpresses just were, but what exactly do you think is going to happen? Do you think that you're going to show up and that she's going to be willing to answer whatever questions you have? You can't be that naive, Mason."

"Listen, I'm going alone and that's it. I'm not going to keep having this conversation with any of you. I'll be back as soon as I can."

Tyler looked at me, worried. "Mason, at least let me tail you."

I shook my head and he let his head down in defeat. "Alright, man. Just be careful, alright? I don't want to have to show up and drain that thing's blood."

I laughed and patted his shoulder. I moved towards the front door. "Thanks man. I'll be fine. Just keep your phone on you. I'll even text you as soon as I'm there."

He gave me an excited thumb up paired with a fake smile and said, "Alright, good luck dude."

XXII.

I drove for about half an hour and finally saw the diner where Seraphina wanted to meet. The building looked like it was straight out of a fifties movie. There were drive-in parking spots with waitresses taking orders out on roller-skates. I parked the car in one of the dine-in only parking spots and walked inside.

I went inside and felt the hairs on my arms tingle. A voice in my head whispered, "Mason, we are here with you. You will not be in harm's way, child."

I let out a sigh of relief and walked towards the back where there was a section of empty booths. A gray-haired lady smiled at me as she handed me a menu. "Hello, darling. My name is Gladys and I'll be your server today. What can I get you to drink today?"

I looked at the menu and then put it down. "I'll have a half sweet, half unsweet tea please."

She gave me a smile and asked, "Will there be another person joining you this afternoon?"

Before I could answer her, a silky familiar voice interrupted. "As a matter of fact, yes. Hello, I'll have a hot orange tea please."

Gladys gave Seraphina a disapproving look. Seraphina played with her fiery red hair. "Oh, and please hold the lemon. I hate lemon."

The elderly waitress let out a huff and tossed a menu down in front of Seraphina as she walked away. Seraphina let out a little giggle. "Someone is a little irritated with me for no reason. Shall I teach her some manners?"

"Leave her alone!"

Seraphina held her hands up in surrender. "Alright, calm down, kidder. Don't let the old lady get you killed."

I laughed. "That's not happening."

Seraphina looked at me closely while continuing to run her long nails through her styled hair. "You're very sure of yourself, little Sheer. I'm surprised you actually came alone. I have to say I am glad, though. I didn't want to get my hands dirty before our meal. I would have hated to have to kill off your little girlfriend or vampire best friend."

I asked, "How do you know Tyler's a vampire?"

She laughed as Gladys brought us our drinks and gave me a smile, while giving Seraphina a sour look. When the waitress left, Seraphina smiled and said, "Oh, sweetie. I know everything. I recommend you get that through that thick little skull of yours."

I took a sip of my tea while she poured a natural sweetener into hers. "Just like I know that you found the original Fitzgerald Brasta."

"How in the hell do you know that? You weren't there!"

She laughed as she took a sip of her hot drink. "Oh my, this is a little too hot. Old bitch probably wanted me to burn myself. Whatever, though. Mason, like I said I know everything. I also know that I really can't hurt you today. I know that your annoying little ancestors are shielding you from me."

I felt my insides go cold as she continued. "Let's get straight to the point, shall we? I had to kill Avant because he was a liability. He was a liability to Malute and quite frankly, he was an annoyance to me. Malute called me here from New York to help him convince you to join his little Shyne army. Do you know what his grand plan is for you?"

I shook my head.

"Look at that, another thing that I know and you don't." She leaned as if she were about to tell me a secret. "You know he wanted to rid the Earth of non-Sheers, right?"

"Yeah, he's a little crazy. That's impossible."

"I don't think it's impossible. It may be a little tough, but not impossible."

"So what are you saying? He wants me to join his Shyne army so I can help him get rid of people like my friends?"

She let out a creepy laugh. "No, he doesn't want to get rid of them anymore."

"What is it that he wants then? I thought you said you were going to get straight to the point. I don't have all day."

Her eyes lit up with fury. "Watch your tone with me, Mason. I'm here to help you out. Haven't you ever heard that saying, don't bite the hand that feeds you?"

"Yeah, I've heard it. What does Malute want me to do for him?"

"He wants to turn them all into hybrids."

"What the hell are hybrids?"

She tapped her long, spiky fingernails on the table. "You're looking at one."

XXIII.

I stared at her for a couple of seconds. She's a hybrid? "I thought you were some type of Fae?"

"Oh, I am. I'm the first of my kind. I'm a hybrid and I've got powers you wouldn't believe."

"How is that possible? How did you become a hybrid? If he created you, doesn't that kind of make you his property? I don't know that I'd call myself his business partner if I were you."

She picked at her nail polish. "Oh, I didn't become a hybrid for his sake. I've got my own agenda, kid. I don't care about turning your friends into hybrids. I actually don't think they deserve this gift."

"So what is it that you want? Why are you telling me all of this?"

"I need Malute to realize he can't get everything he wants. He's jumped bodies for centuries now and the Sheer body he's taken over seems to be the one he wants to make permanent. I thought you wouldn't quite like that idea."

"It's true then? The body he is in, is my dad's? He's actually manipulating my dad's body?"

Before she could respond, a woman shouted on the inside of my head, "Mason, do not listen to the lies this thing is telling you. She is full of deceit. End your meeting with her now."

I closed my eyes to concentrate and then shook my head to shut her up. Seraphina studied me. "Are your little ancestors trying to talk to you?"

I nodded. "They don't want me to talk with you anymore."

"Of course they don't. They don't want me to tell you the truth and that's too bad. Mason, your dad never died. Malute possessed his body."

My lips began to tremble. "Where's my dad?"

"Your real dad is on the other side. The same side where your ancestors are."

I felt my face getting warm with anger. "What do you mean he's on the other side? Why hasn't he contacted me?"

The woman's voice from the inside of my head shouted at me again, "Do not listen to her, Mason!"

My hands were beginning to shake as I felt the thick liquid ooze from them. "Shut up and get out of my head!"

Seraphina smirked at me. "I assume that was for your ancestors and not me, right?"

I nodded. "Keep going. What do you mean my dad is on the other side?"

"When Malute took over your dad's body in that forest, your dad's soul had to go somewhere. He is not dead. He is trapped on the other side and only I know how you can get him back."

"If I got him back, what would happen to Malute?"

"He'd be dead."

"What about my mom? Is she dead, or is she on the other side with my dad?"

Seraphina's eyes dimmed from their normal brightness. "I'm sorry. Malute and his pathetic protégé killed her."

Tears flooded down my cheeks now. "How do I get my dad back?"

"I thought you'd never ask. Let's get out of here, I've got some things to show you."

XXIV.

I followed Seraphina to the familiar abandoned neighborhood and parked my car in front of the house that haunts me in my sleep.

I waited for her at the front door of the home while she fixed her make-up, in the reflection of her tinted windows.

"Are we going to go inside or are you going to be fixing yourself up all day? I've got to get back home before my friends come looking for me."

She glared at me. "Alright, calm down. No need to get your panties in a wad. Let's go inside."

We walked into the home and made our way to the closet where I found the Brasta.

"Why are we here? What did you have to show me? If you know so much, you know that I'm here pretty often."

"You found your family's Brasta here, right?"

I nodded.

"Did you ever happen to think how that Brasta just magically appeared for you?"

"It was a feeling I had. I didn't just randomly notice it. I knew it would be there."

She pursed her lips. "Uh huh. Well, it wasn't just your sixth sense. I planted the book here for you to find. I found it while

I was going through things at Malute's compound. I don't think he's noticed that it's gone yet."

"Why would you do that for me? How did you know that I'd be the one to find it?"

"I need Malute gone. He cannot turn all supernatural beings into hybrids. This should be considered a treasured ability, not some common thing."

"Why exactly did you want to become a hybrid? Like, what sold you on the idea?"

"Did you not see my little disappearing act in the forest? I'm able to do things that every supernatural being can do."

"What do you mean?"

"I can shift into animals like werewolves, I have a vampire's speed, I have affinities like the Fae, I'm in touch with some on the other side and I can dematerialize like Malute."

"Holy shit. You're kidding right? You can do all of that? How? You can talk to people on the other side?"

She gave me a mischievous smile. "I can do a little better than talk with people on the other side. I can go to the other side. I've seen your dad."

"What? That's not possible."

"It is very possible. If you're willing to help me out, I can show you how, too."

"How do I know that you're telling the truth? How do I know that I can trust you?"

"I guess you won't know unless you give me a chance."

Before I could respond to her, my cell phone rang. I looked at the caller ID and saw that it was Benjy calling.

"I'll let you get that. Here's my number, call me when you're ready to see your dad."

She handed me a piece of paper and then with a loud bang, she dematerialized and I was alone.

XXV.

I pulled up to my apartment complex and saw that all of my friends were standing outside. I parked the car in a hurry and ran over to them.

"What's up? What's going on?"

Layla gave me a cold look while my cousin answered me, "We were all about to go looking for you. Why weren't you answering your phone?"

"I only had one missed call from y'all and then my phone died." I held up the screen to show them all the black screen.

Layla gave me an annoyed looked. "Mack, will you go inside to help me pack?"

Help her pack? Where's she going? Benjy put his hand on my shoulder and whispered, "They're all going back home for a couple of days. Mrs. Wrightpress isn't doing too well."

Mackenna, Layla and Geoffrey walked back to the apartment while Tyler, Jayland, Casey and Benjy stayed behind to question me.

"What the hell happened? What did Seraphina want? Does Malute know that you two met up?"

"Y'all have to calm down with the twenty questions. I'll tell y'all everything when we get inside."

I looked up at the sky and pointed at the lightning. "It's about to start pouring and I don't think it'd be good if any of us stayed out here and got sick."

We got inside the apartment and the questions started up almost immediately.

"Look, if y'all want to know everything that happened, give me a chance to tell you!"

Everyone looked at each other, but stayed quiet.

"Okay, well it was really weird. I don't think that Malute knows we met up. And to be honest, I don't think she wants him to know."

Benjy asked, "What do you mean? Why wouldn't she want Malute to know? When she killed Avant she made it clear that she was there because Malute asked her to be. Isn't she just another one of his minions?"

"I don't think so. Seraphina isn't like Avant or the Shyne. Seraphina is a hybrid. She's a mixture of all of us."

Geoffrey's high-pitched voice yelled out, "How the hell is that even possible?"

"I don't know. Benjy, were you able to find out anything while I was gone? Seraphina said that she's able to get in touch with the other side."

My cousin's face went pale.

"She also said that she's seen my dad and can teach me how to see on the other side."

"Mason, what do you mean? That isn't possible. As a Sheer, we're able to communicate with ancestors but we have never been able to visit them."

"Benjy, she's seen my dad! She said that our ancestors are holding things back from us, on purpose. And while I was with her I shut them out. They were trying to interrupt for no reason. I kind of believe her."

"Mason, we don't know anything about her. She literally appeared out of thin air."

"I know! She appeared out of thin air and killed Avant, remember? She didn't hurt any of us. She killed one of them!"

Layla stomped over to me. "Mason, don't be so damn stupid! She killed Avant because Malute told her to. Do you not remember that? How can you trust this girl that just shows up out of nowhere? How do you know if anything she's telling you is true? Don't be such an idiot!"

She looked at Geoffrey and Mackenna. "Are you two ready to get going? I told Mom that we'd be there ASAP."

I blocked her view. "Layla, I know you're mad at me, but don't be crazy. Y'all can't go driving in this weather. It's going to be really bad out."

"Do not tell me what we can or cannot do. We will be just fine."

Mackenna let out a long sigh as she hugged Tyler. "We'll be back in a couple of days."

He leaned down to kiss her as Casey made a disgusted face from across the room.

XXVI.

The next morning, I woke up to Jayland shouting in the next room. I hopped out of bed.

I pulled my t-shirt over my head as I walked into the room. "What's going on? What's happened now?"

Jayland and Casey were arm-wrestling with Tyler.

"Are you guys kidding me right now? I was asleep! Why are you awake already?"

Jayland laughed. "Dude when did you plan on waking up? It's almost noon. We've been up for hours now. You may want to talk to your cousin. We've got some pretty big things on the agenda for today."

"Really? Where is he?"

The three of them pointed at the closed door across the room.

"Hey, can I come in?"

I heard papers ruffling around as Benjy replied, "Ye-yeah, come in!" I opened the door and saw papers with highlighter marks all over them, the floor was covered with books with writing all over the pages and a big map with different colored thumb-tacks on it.

"Um, are you running a CSI lab now or something?"

"Oh, uh, no, sorry I've just had about seven cups of coffee this morning and I've come across some pretty big stuff."

"Okay. Seven cups, really?"

He looked up at me. "Mason, yes seven and I was just about to ask Tyler to bring me number eight."

"That's probably not a good idea. Anyways, what's up with all this?" I pointed at the mess around the room as he followed my hand with his eyes.

"It's my research. I was tossing and turning all night and then I finally just decided to start the day. Mason, you said that Seraphina is a hybrid, right?"

I nodded and cleared a space on the bed so I could sit closer to my caffeine-addicted cousin.

"Yeah, she said that she could shift like a werewolf, had vampire speed, could connect with the other side, has elemental affinities and she could dematerialize like Malute."

"That's so strange. I've gone through the entire Brasta we found and I haven't found anything about her. I have, however, found some things about certain beings that were able to possess bodies and body jump."

"Like Malute?"

"Yeah, just like him. I guess that things like Malute have been around for a long, long time. And I don't think he's the first one to ever be here."

"So how do we get rid of him? How did they get rid of them in the past?"

He pointed at a passage in the Brasta that looked like it was in a foreign language. "The Hood brothers are on their way here, now. I need their help translating this. I think this may explain how to get rid of Malute."

"I hope it does. Do you think we can trust Seraphina?"

"I don't know, Mase. Do you think she'd be willing to meet with all of us?"

"Maybe. She gave me her number I guess I could just call her and ask?"

"Yeah, that'd be good. Maybe you should go to the other room though?"

"Why would I do that?"

He pointed towards the living room. "I put up wards around the bedroom so those with creepy good hearing can't listen in."

Tyler shouted out, "I knew you did something like that! Damn you Benjy!"

I laughed and walked back to the other room. I nervously got the phone off of my nightstand and dialed "S". The phone rang twice then she answered.

"Hello, sweet-stuff. I thought you'd never call. How can I be of service to you today?"

"Do you think that you could come over today?"

"Oh, honey, I'm flattered but I don't think that's a wise idea."

"No, no, not like that. I mean, can you come over and talk with my friends today? I want them to know we can trust you."

"Oh, can you trust me, Mason?"

"I don't know if I can and that's why I want you to meet them. They'll be able to help me figure it out."

She laughed. "What time would you like this meeting to happen?"

"Um, let's say, like three or four?"

"Okay, I guess I can cancel my manicure for you. You owe me. See you in a few hours, sweet-stuff."

As I hung up the phone Tyler walked into the room. "Hey we're going to grab some food. Do you want some? What's up? What's going on?"

"Seraphina is coming over today."

"You've got to be kidding me, right?"

I shook my head.

"Mason, what the hell are you thinking? Why would you invite her here?"

"Benjamin asked me to invite her. I think we can trust her, Ty."

"Mase, if we can't trust her and she knows where we live, don't you think that could be a little dangerous?"

I stayed quiet for a second. "I think she already knows where we live."

"Why do you say that?"

"Because I just invited her and she didn't ask for the address. She just said she'd be here in a few hours."

"Holy shit."

"Yeah, we should probably tell everyone else."

XXVII.

Ty and I walked into the living room where Casey and Jayland were now joined by Ashton, Aden and Benjamin.

Tyler cleared his throat. "Uh, y'all. I think Mason here has something he wants to say."

"Benjy and I were talking just now and we thought it'd be smart for Seraphina to tell you all what she told me yesterday, so I kind of invited her here."

Jayland stood up. "That's a joke, right Mason? You're not that dumb."

I stayed quiet as Benjy defended me. "It was my idea, so leave him alone."

Casey asked, "So you're the dumb one then?"

I shouted, "No one here is dumb! I invited her over because even if I didn't, she already knew where we were. She knows things that no one else does. I think she could be a big help to us."

Ashton asked, "When is she coming?"

"In a couple of hours."

Aden spoke now, "Alright well then it looks like we have a couple of hours to have a Seraphina crash course then, huh?"

The couple of hours went by pretty quickly and felt as if it had only been a few minutes. Seraphina knocked on the door to our apartment. Everyone went pale and tense as I went to let her in.

"Hello, Mason, so nice to see you again, sweet-stuff. I thought your apartment complex would look a little nicer and at least have a valet. This girl actually had to park her own car, how annoying."

She let out a devilish laugh when she saw my friend's facial expressions. "Well hello to you all, too. Just in case you haven't heard, my name is Seraphina."

Benjy stood up. "I'm Benjamin, we all know who you are. There's no need for introductions as I'm sure you know exactly who and what each of us are."

She set her large leather purse down on the table. "Alrighty then. You're just a friendly group of people. I guess you all are all business, huh?"

No one answered her so I invited her to come in and sit down. She took a seat on the love seat and signaled for me to sit next to her. I sat down, uncomfortably, as Benjy started to talk to her again.

"Seraphina, how exactly are you a hybrid? What makes you different from Avant?"

"Don't ever compare me to that thing, Avant. I am a hybrid and I was created, willingly. Malute came to me years ago with a proposition."

"And that was?"

Seraphina clenched her fist. "Sheer, be a little bit more respectful when you talk to me. You may not like me, but you don't know me. I'll answer any questions you have for me, but I will not be disrespected, got it?"

Benjamin's expression relaxed a bit as he answered her. "Alright, I'm sorry about that. I just hope you understand where we are coming from. Until you showed up in the forest the other night, we had never heard about you. We have never heard about hybrids."

"I understand that and again, that is why I am here. I want to get rid of Malute just like you all do. It's in my best interest that he's no longer around."

"Why do you want him gone?" Ashton asked.

"As I was saying, Malute came to me long ago with a proposition to create a hybrid. He already had perfected the Shyne. However, he did not like that they still had so many weaknesses. They were, for the most part, unable to think for themselves. I think that was okay with him in the beginning, but as time went on, he realized an army of Shyne would not be able to complete what he needed them to do."

Benjy questioned, "What exactly is it that he wants? We thought he wanted to either convert all supernaturals into Shyne or to abolish them."

"That was his plan, until I came along. I was already a strong Fae in my community and I was sick of all the rules we had to live by. Why do we all have to hide and try to blend in with mundanes? I know that if they found out we existed, they'd probably freak out a bit, but after all, we're all able to come to an agreement of some kind, so why can't we all just co-exist? It isn't fair that they can walk on this earth out in the open and we're pushed to the shadows."

Seraphina crossed her long legs and continued, "Anyways, I wanted more, so I volunteered to be his first test subject. Turns out, I'm the only one he's been able to create. After a couple of years, Malute disappeared and lost contact with me. I started trials on my own and lo and behold, making hybrids isn't that difficult for me. Now, I've got a community of over one hundred hybrids. I feel that since Malute is back, he wants me to hand over my hybrids to him and that's not going to happen."

I cleared my throat. "So that's why you want to help us? You want us to help you in return, isn't it?"

"I don't really need the vamps, wolves or Fae, but I do need the help of the Sheers. If you all agree to help me, I can show you all how to better connect with the other side."

Aden asked, "How exactly do you think that you can help us do that?"

Seraphina's eyes lit up a bright red. "I know that Sheers can hear their ancestors from the other side, but with my capabilities, you all will be able to walk on the other side. Did Mason tell you that his dad is not dead?"

Tyler looked at me with shocked eyes. "Mason, what the hell is she talking about? How is that possible?"

Seraphina gave Tyler a wicked look. "Aw, is the vampire best friend jealous?"

Tyler let his fangs shows. "Watch it, Seraphina."

She raised her hands in surrender. "I'm not here to start fights. Like I've said, I'm here to help you all, if you all will help me."

We all stayed quiet for a couple of seconds until Benjy asked, "Seraphina, how can we be assured that we can trust you? We want to rid the world of Malute but we also don't really want what you do. How do we know that you won't use us and then try to get rid of us like you are Malute?"

Seraphina raised her hand and silver mist poured out of it and wrapped around her wrist. "Don't you Sheer have promising bonds? Being that I am a hybrid, I am also able to partake in those bonds."

Ashton murmured, "How is that possible?"

Seraphina put her hand back down and her eyes lit up again. "Sheer, if you all agree to help me, you'll learn that there is so much possibility in this world."

Benjamin stood up. "Seraphina, thank you for coming over and explaining your situation to us. I hope you understand that we are not able to take you up on this offer quite yet. We've got a lot to cover with our respective councils."

She stood up and dusted off her hands. "I completely understand. Thank you for having me."

She looked at me. "Mason, will you be a gentlemen and walk me to my car?"

XXVIII.

When I walked back into the apartment, chaos erupted in the living room.

Jayland shouted, "There's no way in hell that we can help that thing! How do we know that she's just not playing us for Malute?"

"We don't know that we can trust her, but why shouldn't we? Remember, she did kill Avant," Ashton said.

Casey interrupted, "She killed him on Malute's orders, did you forget that?"

"Yelling at each other is not going to get anything accomplished here. What if we came up with some sort of mutual agreement?" Benjy chimed in.

Tyler asked, "What are you saying, Benjy?"

"What if we had Seraphina show us how to use our powers to the fullest extent and then helped her a little bit? You know, a little give and take. No one gives too much and no one takes too much. That way we can have somewhat of a buffer in between us."

Jayland let out a frustrated sigh. "Go ahead and make the decision, Benjamin. I know that you already have your mind made up."

"Jayland, don't be upset. I think that Seraphina is telling us the truth. I didn't get any weird vibes from her."

Casey laughed. "So you read vibes now? God, you are pathetic. I can't believe y'all actually think working with that thing can be good for any of us."

Tyler looked at me for confirmation. "Mase, do you really think we can trust Seraphina?"

"I know it's weird, but I think that for right now, it's best that we do. I kind of agree with Benjy, though. We won't need to include her in all of our plans and we shouldn't go telling her any council business, but if it's manpower she needs, I think we've got that."

Tyler nodded and then looked at Jayland and Casey. "If Mason is alright with working with the redhead, so am I."

Ashton and Aden agreed. "We're with them, too."

Jayland and Casey looked at each other and then stood up together. Jayland put his hands in his pockets. "Call the redhead, let her know we're in. But the minute she tries to double-cross us, she's dead."

I shook my head as Tyler asked, "So now that we all sort of agree, who's telling the Wrightpresses?"

Jayland laughed and sat back down. "Oh, this is going to be good. Mason, why don't you call Layla? Put her on speaker while you're at it."

Benjamin interrupted, "Whoa, whoa, whoa. Don't do that Mason. I don't think it's best if the Wrightpresses find out from you. I don't know if you know or not, but you're not Layla's favorite person right now. I think it'll probably be best if I call Geoffrey and let him know what we have decided. They'll be back in another day or so and they'll have to be on board with the plan as well."

Tyler asked, "So you're saying that Layla, Mackenna and Geoffrey are all going to be told that they have to work with Seraphina?"

Benjy nodded.

Tyler groaned, "Ugh, this is going to really suck. I'm not sure I want them to come back so soon now."

Casey laughed. "This is going to be so much fun! I can't wait to see Mackenna's face when Seraphina uses her little fire tricks again."

"Casey, shut your mouth."

Benjamin cut off Tyler and Casey's conversation. "Will you two stop? I'm going to call Geoffrey now. Can you all be quiet for five minutes?"

Everyone stayed quiet as Benjy dialed Geoffrey's phone number.

"Hello? Benjamin? What's up babe?"

"Hey, nothing much. Just here with the gang. We've got some stuff we need to catch you all up on."

"Um, alright should I put you on speaker? The girls are here with me. Oh and Mimaw is too."

Crap. Mimaw is going to freak out, I thought.

"Um yeah, that's fine go ahead and put the speaker on."

Casey and Jayland had a look of joy on their face while Tyler, Ashton and Aden looked anxious.

Geoffrey spoke louder on the phone, "Alright babe, we're all here."

Mimaw's voice broke through the phone, "Hi Benjy and Mason, I hope y'all are doing alright."

Benjy and I responded together, "Hi, Maw."

Benjamin took control of the conversation now. "Okay, so earlier today I told Mason to invite Seraphina over for a meeting. She expressed interest in helping us with some things in exchange for our help to get rid of Malute."

Geoffrey shouted over the jumble of voices from the other end of the line. "Benjamin, please tell me you are kidding! Please tell me that thing was not in the apartment."

"Will y'all please hear me out before you yell at me or get pissed off for no reason?"

Mimaw spoke now, "Benjy, what things could Seraphina possibly help y'all out with? We don't even know what she is or what she's capable of."

"I know that Maw, but after speaking with her today, I feel like she's telling us the truth. Seraphina is a hybrid. She's one of many hybrids that she has created."

Mimaw gasped. "What in God's name is a Hybrid? Oh, Mason. I'm going back up there with the Wrightpresses. It sounds like you really could use me there."

"No, Maw it's okay. We've sort of got things under control."

Layla let out a frustrated sound. "Oh, do you? That's good. What exactly is the plan? How exactly do you have things under control?"

I stayed quiet while Benjamin continued to tell them about the arrangements we made with Seraphina.

"Maw, I sort of agree with Mason when he says we don't need you here. Not because we don't need your help, but because we need your help there, in Midway. I wanted to know if you could help me do a bit of research in regards to some of what Seraphina said to us earlier."

"Alright, Benjy. What exactly did you want me to help with?"

"Well, um, she kind of said that not only could she talk to ancestors on the other side, but she can actually go to the other side."

Maw laughed out loud. "Benjamin, there's no way that's possible. Please, don't tell me that you believe her."

"Well, normally I wouldn't but she kind of said some things that are making me question it. And then Mason said that when he met with her and she was telling him about it, the ancestors were in a riot and were trying to interrupt their conversation, even when he didn't call on them. That kind of struck me as a bit strange, too."

I heard Geoffrey ask Mimaw, "How exactly is it strange for your ancestors to try and protect you all?"

Maw answered him, "Well, it is a bit odd that the ancestors would intervene when they weren't called upon. What else did this Seraphina tell y'all?"

Benjy looked at me nervously and mouthed, "Your dad?"

I took a deep breath and then said, "Well, Maw, she uh, she said that my dad's not dead. She said that she's seen him."

"Mason Connor Fitzgerald, please tell me you do not believe that!"

"Maw, I didn't at first, but when I looked into Seraphina's eyes, I got this feeling."

"What feeling is that?"

"I got this feeling that she was telling me the truth. She made me think, if Malute just jumped into my dad's body, where did my dad go? He couldn't have just disappeared."

"Don't be so foolish. Don't you think that the ancestors would have told us that your dad was over there?"

I mumbled, "Not if they didn't want us to know."

XIX.

Maw shouted back at me, "Mason, what exactly are you insinuating?"

Benjy answered for me, "I don't think he's insinuating anything, but what makes us think we can trust the other side? If we have to question trusting Seraphina, why can't we question our trust of the ancestors? What if there are a couple of bad apples on the other side?"

Geoffrey asked, "Benjy, do you think that it's possible a few of the ancestors are working for or with Malute?"

"I don't know. I mean, I hope none of them are, but we have to be realistic. I think that anything is possible now. A few days ago, none of us knew that hybrids were an actual thing and then all of a sudden, here is Seraphina and her, uh, tribe."

Everyone stayed quiet for a couple of seconds when Maw's voice broke through. "I'm going to ask some other Sheers what they think about this. I just can't imagine not trusting the ancestors. If we can't trust them, who can we trust?"

My cousin sighed. "Maw, that's the thing. I don't think we can exactly trust anyone. Geoffrey, when are you all coming back?"

Geoffrey took a second to respond. "We were going to wait a couple of more days, but now I think that we'll be going back tomorrow."

Benjamin was smiling at the news. "Okay, well, uh, text me later? Maw, I'll call you later or you can call me if you find anything out."

Maw replied, "Alright. You and Mason take care. Oh, and Tyler."

I looked at Ty who was grinning from ear to ear. He shouted, "Miss ya' Maw."

Benjamin hung up the phone and then turned his attention to me. "So what do we do now? How can we prove that at least some of the ancestors are trying to work against us?"

"Do you think that they know what we're thinking at all times? Is that how this works? Can they just come to our minds when we call upon them or can they come at any time?"

Tyler butted in, "That's a good question. I mean, don't you think that if they know what you all are thinking that they're going to try to somehow intervene? Like throw y'all off their tracks?"

Benjy thought for a second. "I don't think that they can technically read our minds. I think that when they tried to interrupt you when you met with Seraphina it was because you had already called on them when you were going to meet her. So they were already kind of on standby, you know?"

I nodded in agreement. "Yeah, you're right. I think that they were only able to interrupt because I had already asked for their help. I know that I was able to shut them out when they were trying to get me to ignore what Seraphina was saying."

Tyler asked, "What do you mean?"

"I mean, I was pretty much able to shut them up."

Jayland spoke for the first time in a long time. "Oh, I bet that really pissed them off. Do you think that since you were able to shut them up that they were kind of blocked from your mind again?"

I nodded again. "Yeah, I think I kind of shut them out completely because after that I didn't hear anything."

Benjy looked at the Hood brothers and then at me. "Maybe we should all try to connect with the other side and see what they know or how they react?"

Ashton pitched in, "That's a good idea. I guess we can try now."

I closed my eyes and then in a matter of seconds, I heard the familiar voices from the other side. They sounded as if they were in a panic. The lady's voice pushed through my mind first.

"Mason, why did you shut us off before? We were there to help you, child. Do you not remember calling upon us for help?"

"Yeah I remember asking for your help but I also remember that I wasn't in any danger. I was just trying to hear Seraphina out."

"You cannot believe anything that comes out of that thing's mouth. She's an abomination and is filled with darkness."

"And how do I know that I can trust anything you say? How do you know we can't trust Seraphina? She's a supernatural being, just like all of us. Isn't it our job, as Sheers, to help the supernatural? Isn't it our job to help them blend in the mundane world?"

"You will not disrespect us! You are just a child! You are lucky we have agreed to help you in the past and that we have helped you gain access to your powers before it was necessary."

"I am thankful you've helped me in the past, but you can't tell me who I can or cannot trust. We can't pick and choose who we help. If we're going to help one supernatural, we need to help them all. If they're going to do bad in the world, well then of course we will stop them, but if they promise that they're not here to do bad, we have to give them the benefit of the doubt."

"That is where you are wrong; we can tell you who to trust. Without trusting us, your powers will weaken and you will no longer have access to channel our powers."

"If I don't have your powers, I'll strengthen my own. If y'all know me so well, y'all know that I don't like being underestimated."

A silken voice stood out from the others now. "You dare to challenge our authority?"

"You have no authority over me. Y'all are dead, I am alive. There's nothing you can do from the other side. Without me using your powers, your powers are useless. Now, maybe it's time you all stop trying to challenge me!"

The familiar lady's voice shouted back at me, "Watch your words, Mason Connor Fitzgerald. We will be in touch."

And after a couple of seconds, there was silence. I looked up at Ashton and noticed that him and his brother were staring at me with widened eyes.

Before either of them spoke, Jayland cleared his throat. "Dude, Mason, you're either the bravest or dumbest Sheer I've ever come across. Do you realize what you have just done?"

I shook my head as Aden continued Jayland's thought. "You just became the other side's enemy."

I looked over at Benjy. "Do you think I should tell Maw about what just happened? If the other side isn't going to help me anymore and if I did somehow become their enemy, don't you think it'd be smart to tell Mimaw before they get to her?"

"Um, yeah you're probably right but let's wait until the Wrightpresses get here tomorrow. I really could use Geoffrey's support in delivering that message. I can't imagine how Mimaw is going to react to what we have to say."

Tyler laughed. "Um, dude, Maw is gonna go crazy. Like, literally. She's going to lose her freaking mind."

XXX.

The next morning my nerves were shot. Tyler didn't let me stop thinking about Layla for a second.

"Dude, do you think that she's still gonna be pissed at you about the whole Seraphina thing?"

"I don't know, man. I mean, I hope not. I think once she understands why I'm doing what I'm doing she'll get it."

Jayland butted into our conversation. "Well, we will have to see about that. Guess who just pulled up?"

I jumped up from the sofa as Tyler let out a creepy laugh.

"Why are you so worked up, Mase? I'm sure Layla will understand your grand plan."

"I'm not worked up. Shut your mouth Tyler."

The door to the apartment flew open as Geoffrey's voice squealed out, "Benjy, baby, I'm home!"

My cousin ran past me in excitement. "Geoffrey oh how I've missed you."

He embraced his boyfriend with a tight hug and a kiss as Mackenna grunted from behind him.

"Eww, will you two get a room already? Nobody worry, an apartment full of guys and I'll carry my own luggage. Thanks though."

Tyler walked up to her and grabbed her bags to ease her annoyance. "Hey babe, I've missed you. How's your aunt doing? Is Maw alright?"

Mackenna hesitantly pushed Tyler away. "Have you showered since I've been gone? I missed you too but God, Tyler, you've seriously gotta keep up with your hygiene."

I laughed out loud as Tyler lifted his arms to smell under them. He made a grimacing face.

Mackenna's attention went quickly from Tyler to me as she heard me laugh. "Are you planning on just standing there or do you plan on going to help my cousin with her bags?"

"Um, yeah, for sure. I didn't know if she wanted to talk to me or…"

"Or what? She probably doesn't want to talk to you but it's going to eventually happen so you might as well rip the bandaid right off."

Tyler pushed me out of the apartment and the moment I stepped outside I could feel Layla glaring at me. I turned around and saw her standing in the parking lot, shaking with frustration.

"Hey, you need some help?"

"I do but I don't think I need *your* help."

"Lay, why won't you just give me the chance to explain things to you?"

"You want to explain things to me after you've already made a plan with everyone and Seraphina?"

The way she said Seraphina was like she was spitting out poison.

"Layla, look, I know you're pissed at me because I am trusting Seraphina, but it's going to be for the best. I'm trusting her but not without keeping my guard up. I'm not stupid!"

"Are you sure about that? Mason, this hybrid thing was able to easily kill Avant. Remember him? Remember how easily he was able to keep up with all of us? Doesn't that freak you out a bit?"

I stepped closer to Layla and reached out to grab her hands.

"I know, she's definitely strong and dangerous, but I believe her. And she is going to show me how I can see and maybe talk to my dad. I need to know what happened the night I thought he died with my mom."

"Do you honestly think that she has seen your dad on the other side, Mason? If she has, how has Mimaw not found out about it? How have none of your ancestors mentioned it to you?"

"I honestly don't have an answer to that. I just know that after last night, not all of the ancestors on the other side can be trusted."

She looked up at me with concern in her eyes. "What do you mean? What happened last night?"

I was about to start giving her the full rundown of the argument I had last night when a girl's voice sent chills down my spine.

"Mason, sweetheart, good morning!"

I squeezed my eyes tightly and then slowly opened them to stare into Layla's.

If looks could kill, I would have been dead the moment our eyes connected.

Layla slowly let go of my hands and I turned around to see Seraphina giving us a devilish smile.

"Good morning, Seraphina. Everyone is inside the apartment if you'd like to head up there."

She looked Layla up and down and then refocused her attention on me. "Alright, well, I guess I better get up there. I don't like being around people who have a clear disdain for me."

I took a long, deep breath and turned to face Layla who was now shaking with anger. "Babe, calm down, it's alright."

"Mason, get out of my way."

She pushed me aside and I felt the air around us start to swirl as if a storm was rushing in.

Seraphina laughed. "Oh, honey. Your little magic tricks don't scare me."

She snapped her fingers and the wind calmed down.

Layla raised her hands and rain started to pour down us, but Seraphina just looked even more amused.

"Baby Fae, stop while you're ahead. Like I said before, none of your magic tricks will scare me."

She snapped her fingers and the rain immediately ceased.

Mackenna and Geoffrey ran up to us. Mackenna stood by Layla before addressing Seraphina.

"What are you doing here? I don't think we summoned any demons today."

Seraphina's eyes glowed a bright red.

"I do not get summoned, although I'm sure some may refer to me as a demon because I can be one of the most terrifying creatures any of you will ever come across."

Mackenna put her wet hair into a ponytail and took off her jacket. "Luckily, not much on this earth scares me."

Geoffrey stood in between his nieces and Seraphina. "Alright girls, why don't we all calm down and get inside before the locals start to wonder what's going on with mother nature?"

None of the girls budged until Geoffrey and I forced them all to start walking towards the apartment. I grabbed Layla's hand and she immediately yanked it away from me.

"Don't touch me, Mason. We will finish talking later."

Geoffrey looked at me with sad eyes and we all made our way up the stairs towards the apartment.

XXXI.

Tyler's eyes widened as soon as he saw Seraphina walk into the apartment ahead of Layla and me. He gave me this 'come sit next to me dude' look, so I walked past the girls and sat next to my best friend.

He whispered, "Dude, what is she doing here? Did you call her? Are you crazy? Like, the girls haven't even settled in."

Benjy started talking to everyone as I answered Ty. "I don't know why she's here. I was talking to Layla outside and then all of a sudden Seraphina was here and well, all hell broke loose."

My cousin cleared his throat. "Mason, would you care to fill the Wrightpresses and Seraphina in on what happened with the ancestors last night?"

I looked around anxiously, wishing I could disappear into thin air. "Um, yeah, sure. I guess."

Seraphina cut me off with a wave of her hand. "No need to fill me in. I know all about the little mishap with your ancestors."

"How the hell do you know about it before we do? Mason, do you care to shed some light on this?" Mackenna asked.

Everyone was glaring at me now and I could feel my face burning bright red. Seraphina let out another creepy laugh.

"Oh, you Fae are all the same. So quick to jump to conclusions. Mason didn't tell me a thing. As a matter of fact that's why I'm here."

Everyone's attention was now back on Seraphina.

She continued, "One of my, let's say, sources, from the other side told me that everyone on the other side is up in arms about the way you talked to them, Mason. No one has ever defied the powerful Sheer ancestors until you. And from what I hear, it's divided the previously united front of the Sheers."

Layla asked, "What's she talking about, Mason? What happened?"

Seraphina answered for me, "Your little boyfriend pretty much accused some of his ancestors of lying or withholding information to him."

Layla, Geoffrey and Mackenna's eyes nearly popped out of their sockets.

"Mason, is this true? Have you lost your mind? If you piss off your ancestors and lose access to their powers, we'll never be able to find or take Malute down." Geoffrey said.

I got to my feet. "Okay, everyone calm down! I'm tired of being told what to do. I'm tired of everyone thinking they know what's best for me or for the situation. None of you, or them, can or will tell me what I should do. I've decided. I'm going to work with Seraphina so I can learn how to visit the other side. I need to get answers and if I can get there, I know that they won't be able to lie to my face."

Benjy looked at me, clearly worried. "Mason, whatever you decide to do, I'll have your back. I may not agree with your every decision but I think you're right. I think that Seraphina can and will help you."

Seraphina twirled pieces of her hair between her fingers. "Aw, how sweet. Cousin Fitzgerald approves of me. We must celebrate!"

Benjamin let out a long sigh. "Don't push it Seraphina. I think you will help him because you want our help with Malute. I don't trust you but I know that we have a common enemy and for now, the enemy of my enemy is my friend."

Ashton and Aden walked towards the center of the room and Seraphina's eyes glowed with excitement.

"Oh, more Sheers? Very handsome ones at that. Why were you two hiding in the corner?"

Aden looked at his brother before answering her. "We've just been taking it all in. We agree with Benjamin. We don't truly believe you're doing any of this for good, but we do believe Mason needs to be able to visit the other side."

Jayland pitched his two cents in, "Look, redhead, you're hot and all, but I've gotta agree with the uptight Sheers on this one. You creep me out but with what you did to Avant, I think you're an ally worth having, even if it is a temporary thing."

Seraphina's eyes somehow looked like they were glowing brighter now. "You all are completely right. I'm not doing this out of the goodness of my heart. I'm doing it solely for selfish reasons. I do not want to make enemies out of any of you and to be frank, I know none of you want to be on my bad side, but we've all got to get rid of Malute."

She looked at the Wrightpresses now. "Are you little Fae in? Can you all put aside the egos and agree to work together for the greater good of this little world of yours?"

Geoffrey looked at his nieces and right before he had the chance to respond, Layla took charge of the conversation.

"Seraphina, I really wish you would quit talking to me as if I am a child. I do not like you and I don't think that anyone here can trust you. Besides killing Avant, what have you done for any one here?"

Seraphina's eyes gave Layla a warning stare. "Have you not been listening to the conversation we have been having? You don't want me to talk to you like you're a kid? Quit acting like one. I'm not here to steal your little Sheer boyfriend away from you. I need his and all of your help to get rid of Malute and Mason wants my help to gain access to the other side. When I tell you all that I have seen Mason's dad, I am telling you the truth.

Not everyone on the other side can be trusted. At the very least, keep your guards up with everyone—not just me."

"Layla, I know it may sound crazy but I kind of agree with them, and with her," Geoffrey said.

He looked at Seraphina and then continued, "If you can teach Mason how to get to the other side, can you teach Benjy, Ashton and Aden too?"

She looked at my cousin and then at the Hood brothers. "Hmm, that shouldn't be a problem. If I help them, will you all agree to help me?"

We looked at each other for a few awkward seconds when Layla spoke again. "I will work with you, Seraphina. I don't like you but I will work with you so I can kill Malute for my dad."

Mackenna's mouth almost hit the ground in shock, and Tyler asked her, "Babe, will you be on board with all of us, too?"

She took a deep breath and then said, "Yeah, I mean, I guess. Whatever. When do we start these little training sessions?"

Seraphina's phone rang and she answered it with an annoyance in her voice. "What do you want?"

I walked towards Layla who gave me a half-welcoming smile.

Seraphina's voice erupted with anger. "What do you mean they're missing? How is that possible? Weren't you watching over them? You know what, I'm on my way. I'll be there soon."

She hung up on whoever was on the line and she looked back around the room. "Somehow, some of my hybrids have gone missing. My guys think the Shyne had something to do with it."

I was holding Layla's hand. "What do you mean the Shyne had something to do with it? Wouldn't your hybrids be a bit smarter than they are?"

Seraphina nodded. "Yup. I don't know. I'm going to check it out and I'll get back to you all. Sheers, let's start the training this weekend. Let me know if anything new happens around here."

I nodded as Seraphina snapped her fingers and dematerialized.

XXXII.

Mackenna made a smacking sound with her tongue and then said, "That thing or girl or whatever she is, is really weird. I don't know that I'll ever be able to get used to that whole disappearing act."

Tyler asked, "Do y'all think we should kind of be concerned about those hybrids missing? Like, I mean, where could they have gone?"

Ashton and Aden started walking towards the door then Ashton turned back to face us and said, "We'll go and see if we can find anything out." He looked directly at Benjy now, "I'll call you if we find anything."

Benjy nodded as the brothers walked out of the apartment. My cousin let out a long sigh and then said, "Well, I think that we should probably start to look for the hybrids. If we find them, we'll probably find the Shyne right there with them."

Tyler added, "And if we find the Shyne, we find Malute."

Geoffrey asked, "Babe, don't you think that you and Mason should start trying to connect to the other side? I think that we should all look for the hybrids while y'all get that down. I know Serahphina said she could show Mason, but maybe y'all can start trying. I think it'd be good."

I looked at Layla and noticed that she was staring at me with tears falling down her cheeks. I put my arms around her. "Lay, what's wrong?"

She tried to push me away and I squeezed her tighter. "Please, don't do that. What's wrong? Talk to me."

"Mason, I'm scared, okay? I don't want to work with Seraphina, I don't want to find the hybrids and I don't want to look for Malute. It all scares me! Malute killed my dad, I hate him but I'm scared of him, okay? Is that what you wanted from me? Did you want to hear me say all of this?"

She was sobbing now and everyone slowly walked out of the apartment. I walked her over to my room and we sat on the bed. "I know it's all scary. I'm scared, too. I'm scared to death."

I felt warm tears on my cheeks and wiped them away quickly. "Lay, this is a lot, I know. If you want to go back to Midway while we do this, I understand."

She pushed away from me. "Is that what you think? You think because I'm scared I want to run away?"

"No, nothing like that, Layla, I just meant…"

She cut me off mid-sentence, "For God's sake, I'm allowed to be scared Mason. I know it seems like I may be jealous of the way Seraphina is with you and I don't know, maybe I am. But, the biggest thing that freaks me out is that she's the first of her kind and she's really unpredictable. She killed Avant because Malute asked her to. She now says she wants us to help her get rid of Malute. Do you really think that if we end up getting of Malute that she'll all of a sudden be a good hybrid? Do you think she won't cause chaos with the other hybrids?"

"I don't think you're jealous of Seraphina, Layla."

I pulled her into my arms again. "You'd be crazy to be jealous of her. You're the only girl I've ever felt this way about. And about us trusting her, again, I don't know. What I do know is that I need to get rid of Malute for what he did to my family and yours. I want to see my real dad, not his body that Malute took over and made his own. I think that if she tried to be this villain with her hybrids, we'd be able to deal with her if and when that happened."

Layla wrapped her arms around my body now and squeezed me tight. "Mason, I love you."

"I…I love you too." I leaned down to kiss her when Mackenna walked into the room.

"I hate to break up this wonderfully disgusting moment of y'alls, but we should probably come up with a plan and start looking for Malute and the hybrids."

XXXIII.

Layla and I followed Mackenna into the living room where Geoffrey, Benjamin and Tyler were sitting around a large map. I saw different areas with red Xs on them and asked, "What's up with the map?"

Geoffrey signaled me to get closer to them. "We've split the map into a few different sections. The red Xs you're asking about are areas we've already searched."

Tyler added, "Yeah, those places are a little creepy and seemed like the perfect hideout for Malute, but there was no sign of him or the Shyne and or hybrids or whatever."

Layla asked, "Are you all sure you weren't being blocked by the wards? If he was there, he could have blinded y'all with wards."

Benjy mumbled, "Well, you're kind of right. If he were there he could put up wards, but Ashton and Aden went with Tyler and there were no wards up."

Geoffrey was twisting the cap to a highlighter and then pointed out the different circled areas on the map. "These sections that are circled are areas we want to take a closer look at. There have been reports of missing people in nearby neighborhoods and I think those kidnappings have Malute written all over them."

Mackenna asked, "So, what are we waiting for? Let's go look for this guy and end him! I'm sick of playing hide-and-seek with him."

Benjy laughed. "Calm down, Mackenna, y'all are going to go look at a few of those places in a bit. Mason and I are going to try to visit the other side and see if we can spark some nerves before Seraphina digs in and teaches Mason to physically visit."

Tyler let out a long yawn. "Dude, I wish I could take a nap. I'm freaking exhausted."

Mackenna hit him on his ribs. "You're a vampire, Tyler. Do you even need sleep?"

He rubbed his stomach, "Ouch, babe. Chill out! I don't really need to sleep but I love sleeping. So yes, I wish I could take a nap."

We all started laughing. Just then there was a knock on the door. Layla went to open the door but Seraphina pushed past her and smiled at me. "Alright, we've got to find Malute. He's got my Shyne. Are you ready to visit the other side, kid?"

XXXIV.

Mackenna gave Seraphina a fake smile while Benjy asked, "Seraphina, how do you know Malute took them? What's happening?"

She started to chip at her nails. "He left me a little note. You know him, he loves a good note. It makes me sick to be quite honest."

Geoffrey grabbed his jacket from the sofa nearest him. "Alright, let's get going. We have got to find Malute. I don't know what he's doing with the Shyne and hybrids, but humans are starting to go missing and we've got to do something about it."

Layla, Mackenna and Tyler all followed Geoffrey's lead and got their coats on. Layla walked over to me and wrapped her arms around me. She didn't have to tell me. I could feel the love vibrating off her, and I know she could feel mine. She kissed me and then just stared at me.

Mackenna made a disgusted sound, "Okay, we get it. Y'all love each other. Let's go Lay."

They headed out of the apartment and as Layla turned to close the door she winked at me and stuck her tongue out at Seraphina.

Seraphina laughed. "Your little Fae girlfriend is extremely brave and a bit immature."

"I know and I love her for it."

Benjy broke up our conversation. "Alright Seraphina, let's get to it. What do we have to do?"

She took off her coat and threw it on the kitchen table. "So, I know y'all are able to connect with the other side already. I also know that y'all, especially you, Mason, communicate pretty regularly with some of your ancestors."

I nodded and she continued, "Now, visiting the other side doesn't take much more. You just have to know how to feel for the, let's say, door."

I asked, "What do you mean feel for the door? When I talk to the ancestors I kind of just feel like I'm closing my eyes and hearing them in my head."

She clapped her hands together. "When you hear them you just have to focus on seeing them. The fact of the matter is that when you are communicating with them, you are already on the other side."

Benjy added, "That makes sense. I mean, I know that when we reach out to the ancestors on the other side, they're able to see us and are able to see who we are with."

Seraphina nodded with a devilish grin. "Ten points for you, Benjamin. You're catching on."

My cousin blushed and asked, "Do you think that we are unable to see the ancestors because they don't want us to?"

I chimed in, "You mean, like maybe they're putting up a ward against us?"

Seraphina twirled a piece of her hair between her fingertips. "I swear, you Fitzgerald Sheers are quite impressive. You are both right. The ancestors on the other side have wards not only blocking you all from seeing them, but from most of this world seeing them. I can see them because I've perfected it with my wonderful talents. Being a hybrid, I'm a little more powerful than your little ancestors would like me to be. I don't think they even know that I've been on their side."

My cousin demanded, "Alright, well then show us how to do it. We have to see Mason's dad. We have to know you're not lying to us."

She took a deep breath and signaled for us to hold onto her hands. "Alright, alright. Calm down, Sheer. Buckle up, boys."

XXXV.

We grabbed onto her hands and I felt the familiar warm liquid form in my palm. I closed my eyes and immediately felt a hot, electric pulse go up my arm.

I was about to open my eyes to see what was causing the spark when Seraphina said, "Keep your eyes shut and focus on the other side. Imagine yourself in a dark room trying to feel for a door."

I squeezed my eyes shut tighter and did what she said. A couple of seconds later I felt it. I felt a hot door handle.

I whispered, "Benjy, Seraphina, I found it! I found the door."

I felt my cousin's hand around my arm. "Open it, I'm right behind you."

I opened the door and a bright light flooded the dark space we were in. I rubbed my eyes to adjust my vision and then turned around to see my cousin doing the same.

"Mason, how did you find the door handle? I was trying to but I just felt like I were touching a wall the entire time."

"I don't know how I did it really. I just closed my eyes, reached out and a second later my fingers touched the handle. It was really hot."

Seraphina whistled and broke up our conversation. "Hello, earth to the Sheers. Are you two ready to find Mason's dad or what?"

I turned back around and saw the she was sitting atop a tall tree that was covered with yellow, orange and red leaves. She hopped down with little effort and then wiped her hands on her jeans.

"We need to get going. I don't want the wrong person to find us before we find your dad. I really don't want to pick a fight with some dead Sheer."

We started to jog towards a street filled with two-story houses that all looked exactly the same. They were all bright blue with white trim. All of the yards looked identical and mailboxes were labeled with numbers.

We kept up our pace until we came to a halt in front of a house that was numbered 23. I looked at Seraphina. "Who lives here? What do we do?"

"One of the few ancestors I know we can trust on this side live here. You two should go in, she's expecting y'all. I'll be on look-out."

I turned to my cousin. He looked as confused as I felt. We started to walk up to the house when I heard a raspy, high-pitched voice from inside say, "Boys, come in, hurry up now."

I opened the screen door and led the way into the home. As soon as we walked in I was hit by a familiar smell. My cousin whispered, "It smells like Mimaw's kitchen, huh?"

I nodded and then saw a small gray-haired lady with glasses standing in front of us. She looked eerily similar to Mimaw. She smiled at us and said, "Now, boys, that's no way to introduce yourself to your great grandma."

Benjy asked, "You're Mimaw's mom?"

The short lady smiled and held her arms open. "Give me a hug, you two. That Seraphina woman said that she was going to bring y'all here, but I didn't believe her. I don't know who or what to believe anymore but it's a great day when I get to see my great-grandkids."

When she finally released us from the tight hug, I asked, "How long have you been here? How do you know Seraphina?"

"I've been here quite some time, my boy. I've been watching over you and your Mimaw for what seems like an eternity. It feels so good to have you here with me. I've known Seraphina for a few months now. I ran into her when she first came to this side."

Benjy questioned her, "So she hasn't been lying to us? She actually saw Mason's dad? He's really stuck here? Are some of the ancestors really working with Malute?"

Mimaw's mom started walking towards a back room and we instinctively followed her. "I know this is hard for you two to believe, but yes. Mason, your dad is here and that Malute thing has taken over his body. I'm also afraid to admit that some of our ancestors on this side are indeed in cahoots with that Malute charcater. I've tried to contact your Mimaw from this side but it's like there's a ward blocking our connection. There's no way someone from this side has that kind of power."

I felt tears running down my face now. "Where's my dad?"

She fidgeted around with some ornaments she had on a tall wooden bookshelf. "I guess you could say he's on the other side of town. I haven't been able to talk to him for some time now. I think they know Seraphina has been to this side."

My cousin put his hand on her delicate shoulder. "Who exactly are 'they'?"

My great grandma looked at both of us with a frightened look. "They are the leading Sheers on this side. They control everything. They say who can come to this side and they say who is no longer welcome on this side. They're kind of like the council here."

"Where is this council? I want to talk to them. I have to talk to them. I need them to know that they're on the wrong side. I need to know what they get out of helping someone like Malute."

Seraphina came running into the room. "You guys, we've got company approaching. There's a herd of pissed-off Sheers walking this way."

Maw's mom instantly went pale. "Y'all have to get out of here! They'll keep you here forever! They'll turn you over to *him*!"

My cousin tried to drag me out of the room as I yelled, "I'm not afraid of them! Let them come here!"

"Mason, you might not be afraid of them but she clearly is," Benjy snapped.

I looked at my great grandma again and saw that she looked like she was about to faint. My cousin was holding onto my arm again and I yanked it free. "We'll go to them then. They don't have to know we came here to see her."

I ran out of the house with Seraphina and Benjy. We headed towards the next street corner. We made it two blocks from my great-grandma's house before we saw a group of Sheers walking towards us.

A lady with bleached blonde hair stood at the front of the group. She lifted her hands and the Sheer mist poured from them towards the sky. She looked like she was vibrating in place. She shouted out, "How dare you come here! This is no place for the living!"

I stepped closer to her and lifted my hands to match hers. My powerful mist overshadowed hers and I saw her eyes blink with fear. "Where is my dad?" I demanded.

A short round bald guy laughed. "We have no idea who you're talking about!"

Seraphina was at my side now and her red hair started swirling around her. From the corner of my eye, I saw her red eyes were glowing. "I wouldn't try anything funny, baldy," she said, her voice menacing.

The rest of the group standing in front of us gasped. The bald guy asked, "How did you get here? You are not a Sheer!"

Seraphina smirked. "You've got that right. Like I said, I wouldn't try anything funny, baldy."

The blonde lady raised her hands higher and I noticed her Sheer mist turn almost black. I whispered to my cousin who was standing behind Seraphina and I, "Doesn't that look kind of like Malute's mist?"

My cousin responded in a low voice, "Yeah, it kind of does."

The lady got our attention with her booming voice. "Mason Fitzgerald, you have been shunned from this side. We will not help someone who defies nature and aligns themselves with someone like her."

"You are no one to shun me. I am a Fitzgerald Sheer, I am from the strongest Sheer family of all time. You trying to shun me is a joke. Funny, though, that you say I am aligning myself with someone like her. What about y'all? I know that you're working with Malute!" I spat at her.

The group of Sheers started to mumble and murmur amongst themselves, then the bald guy spoke again. "You have no proof that we are working with him. You may be of the Fitzgerald bloodline, but you have no authority on this side!"

My cousin pushed through Seraphina and I. "Enough with the empty threats!" He threw his hands towards them and his bright, silver mist surrounded their group. "Where is Mason's dad? We are not leaving without him."

The blonde woman waved her hand and her dark mist pushed my cousin's aside. "You three are leaving, whether you like it or not. And you are not taking anyone with you."

Seraphina's eyes glowed brighter. She snapped her fingers and tossed a small flame at the group. A tall, brown-haired woman shouted in pain and started rolling on the ground.

Seraphina jumped up and with both hands, threw a ball of fire at the group. The group's leader met her midair and blocked the fireball with a dark, black, oil-like ball of her own. She screamed out, "If you do not leave right now, I will make sure that Mason's dad endures a long and miserable life with us!"

I closed my eyes and felt my body instantly start to heat up with anger. I could feel the strong Sheer mist growing inside me. It started from the bottom of my feet, seemed to move up my legs, into my stomach and then into my chest. When I opened my eyes again, my arms were stretched out and a bright silver mist was wrapped around the small group of Sheers. I squeezed my palms and it felt as if I were grabbing onto a rope. The group of Sheers started to cry out in pain. The bald guy's voice stood out from the others.

"Let us go! I'll show you where your dad is! Please!"

I squeezed them tighter and saw that Seraphina's eyes were still glowing with anger. "Where is my dad?" I demanded.

The brown-haired woman cried out, "Please! Let us go! You're going to kill us!"

I squeezed them tighter. "You all are not living Sheers, remember? You're already dead. Now, where is my dad?"

The bald man cried out again, "He's in house 97! Malute has wards around the house that no Sheer can pass through!"

Seraphina whispered, "Good thing I'm not a Sheer. Let's go."

Benjy asked, "What do we do with them? What if they try to stop us again? What if they get hold of Malute?"

I smiled. "I've got an idea. Benjy, I'm going to hold them in place. While I do that, can you put up wards around them? It should take them a while to break through them."

"Good one, cuz."

XXXVI.

Benjamin set up the wards and we ran towards house 97. As soon as we passed house 92, we hit Malute's wards. The wards were as black as night.

Seraphina made a whistling sound. "I hate the guy but his wards are really good. It's a bit annoying."

My cousin laughed, "Yeah, if he wasn't such a murderous prick I'd give him props. But the whole kidnapping-people-and-murdering-them makes it all a bit irrelevant. Mason, you've got through his wards before, do you think you can do it again?"

"I don't know. I think that the last time I got through his wards I had the ancestors' help. After what we just did to them I think we're kind of on our own."

Seraphina walked towards the ward and put her palm on it. "Damn, I don't know that I'll be able to break through. This bad boy has a few layers to it."

I closed my eyes and tried to envision myself on the other side of the wards. Come on, Mason, I told myself, you can do this. You've done it before. Get to your dad. He needs you.

I opened my eyes and saw that I was standing in front of house 97. I looked back and could see my cousin and Seraphina looking around for me. I felt a warm liquid running down my face and as I wiped it away, I saw that it was blood.

I heard a voice that made every hair on my body stand up. It was a voice I've only heard in my recurring nightmare. It was my dad.

"Mason, Mason, is that you?"

I slowly turned around, afraid of what I was going to see.

I instantly fell to my knees. My dad looked eerily like me; he ran towards me with tears running down his face. "Mason, it is you! How did you find me? You haven't passed on have you?"

I stayed quiet as he wrapped his arms around me and I cried until he shook me. "Mason, are you okay?"

"Ye-yeah. I just can't believe it. You're here. You're alive. I thought that you were dead. I thought you killed Mom. All this time…"

He hugged me tighter and cried out loud, "I could never do that to your mom, Mason! I have always loved her more than life itself. Malute knew that. That's why he had her turned away from here, she was shunned and he kept me here as a prisoner. He wanted us apart for all eternity."

"You've got to come back with me, Dad. I don't know what I'm doing. I am so scared! I need you!"

"I've been trying to break out since the day I got here, Mason. I can't break through the wards. From what I gather, no Sheer can. The others have been trying to help me but they've all failed."

"No, they're all liars. They're working with Malute. I can't explain it right now, but I can get us out of here, Dad. Grab my hand."

My dad's warm hand was in mine and I closed my eyes.

XXXVII.

When I opened my eyes, I was lying in my bedroom and Layla was standing over me.

"Benjy, Geoffrey, get in here! He's awake!"

I tried to sit up and she gently pushed me back down. "Don't move too much, babe. I don't want you to hurt yourself."

"How did I get here? Where's my dad?" How long have we been back?"

My cousin and Geoffrey walked into the room. Benjy leaned in and hugged me. "You had us all so worried, cuz!"

"Where's my dad? Did I get him out from the other side?"

He nodded. "Yes, you did. I think that when you broke through the wards the second time, it took too much energy from you. You collapsed and we had to carry you back. Thankfully, your dad was able to help us."

"Where is he?"

"He's with Mimaw right now. They're with the Hood brothers looking into another mundane death."

"How long was I out?"

"You've been asleep for about a week."

"What the hell? A week! How did y'all not take me to a hospital?"

Mackenna laughed as she came into the room with Tyler.

Tyler looked relieved. "Mase, dude, I am so happy to see you! I mean, I've seen you passed out for a week, but I'm happy to see you conscious."

"I'm glad y'all had enough faith in me to wake up from my death coma."

Seraphina's voice came through from behind my group of friends. "Don't be so dramatic, Mason. I was playing nurse the whole time. You know my whole hybrid powers are limitless."

Layla smiled and then leaned in to kiss my cheek.

I hugged her and asked, "How did Mimaw get here? Did she come with your mom?"

Layla shook her head. "No, my mom went to Chicago to be with the rest of our family when Maw came over here. Mimaw came the second she heard that you had found your dad. She couldn't believe it. They've been sleeping in here the entire time, waiting for you to wake up."

Mackenna snorted. "Yeah, they've been waiting for you to wake up and go figure, the minute they're gone, you decide to rise from the dead, Lazarus."

My stomach growled and the room filled with laughter. My cousin asked, "What do you feel like eating? Sounds like you could possibly be hungry. We'll go get you whatever you want."

"How about Italian? And, um, Chinese?"

Layla poked my stomach. "Dang, fatty."

Geoffrey hugged my cousin. "Alright, Mason, we'll go get you both. And we'll call Mimaw to let her know you're awake while we're at it."

"Thanks, Geoffrey."

As Geoffrey and my cousin left the room, Seraphina moved closer to me. "I hope you're all caught up on your sleep. I'm pretty sure we've found Malute's little Shyne warehouse."

"Seriously? Yeah, I'm good to go! I can't wait to kill those bastards."

Tyler laughed. "Calm down, dude. You just got up. No need to go GI Joe right now. We've got a little time. Casey and Jayland have found a couple of Shyne hotspots. I think they're close to finding the missing hybrids, too."

"Yeah, I didn't really want to wait for you to wake up from your beauty sleep to attack the warehouses, but your dad made a good point. He said if we attack too soon, Malute will probably just move the other Shyne and hybrids again. We want to find all of the locations and then attack them at the same time," Mackenna said.

I slowly sat up. "That's good thinking."

I looked at my best friend. "Ty, I can't believe it. My dad is alive."

"I know, man. He's alive and he's a total badass."

"Is he really?"

Tyler nodded. "Yeah, he's really smart. Unlike you."

"Ha ha."

"No, seriously though, he's a really cool guy."

"Have y'all already told him about the ancestors working for Malute?"

"Yeah, Redhead over here and your cousin filled him in. He couldn't believe it."

Seraphina cleared her throat. "I'd watch myself if I were you, baby vampire."

She glared at him and then continued, "Your dad was telling us how the Sheers on the other side kept trying to break through the wards, but when we told him what we knew about them, it changed his perception on things. He thinks that instead of them trying to help him out, they were actually adding onto Malute's wards. They were literally reinforcing his jail cell."

"I wish I could kill every single one of them. I hate that they're already dead. How can we get rid them from the other side? People like Mimaw's mom are living there in fear. That's not right."

"The Hood brothers are working with your Mimaw and dad to find a solution for that. I'm pretty sure we can all think of something clever. Hell, you practically held them hostage with the grip of your bare hand."

Tyler asked, "Dude, are you serious? That's freaking awesome! My best friend is a total badass."

"Yeah, thanks, but it wasn't as glamorous as she's making it seem."

XXXVIII.

An hour later our apartment was filled with people. Jayland, Casey, Mimaw, and Dad joined us for dinner.

My dad took a seat next to me with his full plate. "Well, it looks like us Fitzgerald men have the same appetite."

Mackenna teased, "Mr. Fitzgerald, Mason's metabolism is working quite fast still, if I were you I'd slow it down. A second on the lips isn't worth a lifetime on the hips."

Mimaw scowled, "Mackenna, now why don't you mind your business and fetch us all some cold drinks."

Layla laughed and shouted after Mackenna, "Get me a tea, please!"

Her cousin turned around and flipped her middle finger at her.

My dad smiled and then said, "No need for any of you to call me Mr. Fitzgerald; Manuel will be fine."

Layla smiled at my dad as Mackenna handed her a glass of tea. My dad asked, "So, Jayland, were you and Casey able to track any other warehouses down?"

Jayland put his fork down. "We have a total of six locations now."

Casey added, "We're not really sure what's inside of them because he has wards up, but that's how we were able to tell they were his warehouses."

Geoffrey turned and looked at my dad. "Mr. Fitzgerald, I mean, Manuel, when you were on the other side, did you ever communicate with the other Sheers?"

My dad took a sip of his drink before answering. "Well, the wards were up and we weren't able to talk in person, but I did have a phone that they'd call. They would assure me that they were all going to continue to try to get me out."

Seraphina chuckled, "So, those little sneaky traders were helping Malute keep you hostage while they led you on to believe that they were there to help you? What a joke!"

My dad's face turned red with frustration. "Yeah, I guess so."

I asked, "How can we get rid them from the other side? They don't deserve to be there. They need to be put in hell along with Malute."

Tyler added, "Yeah, those Sheers are no better than Malute. If they wanted to work for him so bad, they won't mind spending eternity with him."

Mimaw chimed in, "Now, you boys need to settle down. I know that you're all upset, and God knows I am too. The ancestors will get what's coming to them. Let's focus on Malute for now. They're not going anywhere. They're stuck where they're at."

Maw turned her attention to Jayland. "When do you think we'll be ready to attack Malute's warehouses?"

Jayland slowly swallowed his food and then looked at all of us. "I think that now is a good time. We have six of his locations and if we all split up, we'll be able to attack them all at once."

Casey added, "If we attacked the warehouses all at once, that would really throw him for a loop. We can pretty much bet that it would cause Malute to come out of hiding."

Maw asked, "Do y'all think he'll lash out and kill more mundanes?"

The room fell silent and we all stared at each other.

Seraphina broke the silence. "I don't know if he'll kill more mundanes, but if we are able to take down six of the warehouses, I know he'll want to kill something."

Mackenna added, "Or someone."

Mimaw's eyes filled with worry. I decided to ask what everyone was wondering. "So, when do we do this?"

XXXIX.

The next morning my friends and I slept in as we prepared to attack Malute's warehouses.

Maw's voice woke me from my dreams. "Boy, do you plan on sleeping until next year? You need to get up!"

Having Mimaw around again to wake me up is something I've really missed.

I made a grunting sound. "Yes ma'am. I'm up."

She tore the blankets off of me. "You're not up, until you're up and out of bed! Layla's helped me prepare a big meal and you're the last to come and eat."

"Layla helped you cook? Are you sure the food is edible?"

"Mason Connor Fitzgerald, don't be so rude! I'm not gonna tell you again. Get out of this bed and get dressed. We'll be waiting for you in the living room."

I wiped my eyes, put some pajama pants on and headed to the living room.

"Hey y'all. I guess I was a little more tired than I thought."

Layla walked over to me with a plate loaded with pancakes. "I heard you making fun of my cooking. Eat this and then tell me I'm not the best cook, ever."

Maw turned her head disapprovingly. "Now, young lady, I told Mason not to be rude but you should try not to be so confident in those skills of yours."

The room filled with laughter as I started to eat the stack of cakes.

Tyler sat next to me. "Dude, eat up. Tonight's going to be a long night."

"Yeah, I know. I'm pretty anxious, man. What if we do the wrong thing? What if we take down these warehouses and there's something bigger we're missing?"

"The only thing bigger than burning down these warehouses full of those sick Shyne, would be taking Malute down. You know he's going to come out and play tonight. He won't be able to resist."

"Let's hope so. I'm sick of this hide-and-seek game we've been playing with him."

I put my fork down and took a drink of my milk. "Ty, last night before I fell asleep I was thinking of a way we can get rid of the ancestors from the other side."

He leaned in closer to me so the others wouldn't hear what we were talking about. "Oh, you're for real about this, huh?"

"Yeah, what they did to my dad. What they're doing to the good ancestors. It's not right."

"Yeah dude, they're pretty messed up. I agree with Maw though, let's deal with Malute and then we'll figure something out with those losers."

Layla and Mackenna sat on opposite sides of Tyler and me.

Mackenna began to brush her hair violently. "I'm really sick of sharing two bathrooms with all of these people. It's borderline abuse."

Layla laughed. "Oh, the horror. Sharing a bathroom…the world as we know it is coming to an end!"

Her cousin stopped brushing her hair. "Don't start with me today, Layla. I can't wait until this is all over. We can go home and have our own bathrooms again. And we won't have to see any of them for a long time."

She pointed at Seraphina, Jayland and Casey. Seraphina's eyes lit up as she walked over to us. "I thought I heard my name. Is there something I can help you with, Mackenna?"

Mackenna stood up. "Nope, nothing. And just so you know, I'm not afraid of you."

Seraphina snapped her finger and a small flame appeared.

Mackenna snapped her fingers and a small, round orb was floating above her palm. "Don't forget, you're not the only one with magic powers, lady."

Mimaw slammed a pan on the kitchen counter. "Will you two put those things away and save the hate for tonight? We have a common enemy and I need you all to remember that!"

Mackenna and Seraphina kept their eyes on each other, but the flame and light disappeared.

Tyler let out a long sigh and whispered, "Mase, you've got to admit, that was real hot."

Mackenna continued to stare at Seraphina but still managed to hit Tyler with her balled-up fist.

He rubbed his shoulder. "Ouch! Sorry, babe."

Seraphina smiled at Mackenna now. "I'm sort of impressed with you. You didn't even think twice about defending yourself against me. Even after seeing what I'm capable of."

Mackenna reluctantly returned the cease-fire smile. "I'm not afraid of anyone in this world. Or the next."

Seraphina reached out to shake Mackenna's hand and all of us held our breath.

Mack shook her hand and then continued to brush her hair as she sat back down. "Alright, I guess we should all get ready to go, huh?"

XL

A few hours later we were all dressed and met outside the apartment complex to talk about our strategy for the night.

Benjy took lead of the conversation. "Alright, so we know that there are six warehouses we want to take down tonight. We need to split up, so we can try to take them all down around the same time. Geoffrey and I came up with these maps and groups earlier this morning."

Geoffrey handed each of us a small map and saw there were three groups highlighted on the map.

Casey asked, "Uh, how are three groups of us going to take out six warehouses?"

Geoffrey answered her, "Well, we thought we would be more efficient in bigger groups and when we set off the first couple of warehouses, we're pretty sure Malute will be alerted."

Benjamin continued, "We grouped each warehouse by location so we'll all be within two to three minutes of the next warehouse. It'll be a pretty cool domino-effect."

He started to read off the groups, "Geoffrey, Casey, and Ashton will be with me. Manuel, Aden, Jayland and Seraphina will go to their warehouses together. Tyler, Mackenna and Layla, y'all are gonna be with Mason."

Layla squeezed my sweaty palm. "It's gonna be okay."

Mackenna added, "Girl, it's going to be fun! Let's burn these suckers down!"

I looked at Mimaw. "Where are you going to be? I don't want you in town for this. I don't want Malute to try to get you for revenge."

Maw gave me a comforting smile. "I'll be just fine, baby. I'm flying to Chicago to be with Mrs. Wrightpress as soon as I leave here."

I let out a long sigh of relief. "Thank God."

Mimaw walked closer to me and kissed me on the forehead. "I hope God watches over you, baby. I hope he watches over all of y'all. Call me as soon as it's over, please."

I nodded and felt warm tears fall from my eyes.

XLI.

Layla, Mack, Tyler and I pulled up to our first warehouse. I immediately saw the black ward that surrounded the building.

I mumbled, "Damn, this is going to be a little tiring."

Tyler laughed. "Dude, we can just walk inside."

"Um, no, we can't. There are wards up. You don't see them?"

"Uh, no, man. I just see the front door."

Layla added, "Mason, we can't see the wards. Only you can."

"How did Casey and Jayland find it then?"

"They have a unique sense of smell. I'm pretty sure they just smelled the rotting Shyne in there."

Mackenna covered her mouth. "That is freaking disgusting. Come on, let's get this over with. Mason, you've got to get the wards down, quick. Layla and I will have tons of fun burning this sucker down."

We all got out of the car and walked over to the building that was currently surrounded by thick, black wards.

I closed my eyes and took a deep breath as I lifted my palms in the air.

I heard Tyler say, "Do your thing, man. I'll be the lookout."

Instead of trying to communicate with the ancestors like I previously had, there was one ancestor that I wanted to call upon specifically.

I mumbled, "Grandma Fitzgerald, can you hear me? I need your help. I need your help with the Brasta from your spirit world."

There was silence so I continued, "Please, hear me and help me. I can't trust anyone on that side besides you."

After a minute of silence, I was just starting to lose hope when I heard her smooth, calming voice.

"Mason dear, I am here. I have the Brasta. Keep concentrating on the wards."

I felt a vibration from the bottom of my toes travel up my body and out through my palms. I opened my eyes and saw a rainbow mist push into the dark wards. Suddenly a small hole appeared and it started to expand.

My great-grandma's voice came through to me again. "Mason, tell your friends to burn it down, now!"

I shouted, "Mackenna, Layla do it! Burn it, now!"

I heard a loud clap of thunder as I glanced at Layla. She had her hands up and suddenly lightning bolts began to hit the building.

Mackenna clapped her hands together and then slowly pulled them apart. There was a fire orb that grew steadily as she pulled her hands away from each other. I started to feel the heat from her fireball and then she did it. She released the huge fireball at the warehouse and the building immediately caught on fire.

Layla lifted her hands and I could now see a bright blue and white light in her hand. She threw her hands forward and I jumped back, shocked.

"Wow! When did you learn how to do that?"

She smiled at me. "You mean, when did I learn how to throw a lightning bolt?"

I didn't get to answer her because Tyler shouted, "We've got to go! Someone is coming!"

We all ran back towards the car and headed to the second location. Layla was driving us and I checked my messages. I had two texts. One from Benjy and the other from Seraphina. They both said "One Down."

I clapped my hands with excitement. "We're almost done! They did it!"

Tyler asked, "They got their buildings down, too?"

I nodded and he screamed out, "Hell yeah! Let's do this!"

Our second warehouse was only a couple of blocks away and when we pulled up, I noticed that there weren't any wards on this building.

"Uh, I don't know if we should get off right now."

Mackenna huffed. "What do you mean? We're almost done! We just basically have to rinse and repeat. We are literally that close to me getting back to my own bathroom!"

Layla threw her phone at her cousin. "Shut up, Mackenna. Mason, what's going on? What should we do?"

"I don't know. There aren't any wards up around this building. That's a bit weird, don't you think?"

Tyler answered, "Yeah, that's definitely weird. Call Benjy. See what he thinks we should do."

Before I could call my cousin, I had an incoming call from Seraphina.

I answered it on speaker phone. "Hey, Seraphina, we're at our second location. There are no wards up. What do we do?"

"Don't go in! We're on the way. We're all done with ours. Your cousin just called me, he's going to meet us there too."

I hung up the phone and looked at everyone. "I guess we should wait for them. If there are no wards up, I don't think we should just burn it down.

Maybe, we should all go in. Maybe Malute's here?"

Mackenna protested, "Or maybe Malute wants us to go in so we can fall into his little trap."

Layla defended me. "Let's just wait for the others. We can all decide what to do as a group."

XLII.

A few minutes later the whole gang was at our second warehouse location. Benjy and my dad walked over to me as I got out of the car.

My dad asked, "Mason are you alright? How did your first building go?"

I smiled and hugged him. "I'm fine, it was awesome! Grandma Fitzgerald helped me! I've always been able to go head to head with Malute when the ancestors helped me but I obviously couldn't call on them this time. But she had her Brasta and that really just put me over the edge."

I looked at my cousin who was beaming with happiness. "My Sheer mist was that cool rainbow mist. Remember when you were first teaching me to connect with the spirit world at Windsor Park?"

"Yeah, of course I remember. Mason, I'm so proud of you. You've come a long way in such a small amount of time. I'm really in awe of you."

My dad added, "I agree with Benjy. You are an extraordinary Sheer, Mason. Your mother would be so proud."

Geoffrey broke up the sentimental moment. "I hate to disrupt this family reunion, but we really need to decide on what to do."

I turned to face my group of friends. "When we got here, I noticed that there weren't any wards surrounding this warehouse. The first building was completely hidden behind them and I thought instead of burning this building down, we should probably go in."

Mackenna huffed. "And then I brought it up to this genius, that if we go in, we could just be falling for one of Malute's traps."

Layla added, "Hence, the reason we're all standing outside of this building."

Ashton looked at his brother and then spoke up, "It is weird that this building doesn't have wards up. The warehouses we took down were also covered in Malute's dark wards. Hell, I almost couldn't break through one."

Aden asked, "What if half of us went inside and the other half stood outside as back-up?"

My cousin, thinking it over, took a second to respond. "I think that's the best choice. Why don't me, Mason and Manuel go in?"

Ashton questioned him, "You think it's a wise decision for all of the Fitzgerald Sheers to go in together?"

"Yeah, maybe that's not the best plan. What if Mason, Seraphina and me go in? The three of us could take on an army." My dad suggested.

Seraphina's eyes lit up with excitement. "Oh, yes. That would be a lot of fun! Let's do this."

XLIII.

Seraphina led the way inside the building and as soon as we got inside the building, the stench of Shyne hit us.

She covered her nose and mouth. "Good lord, they are disgusting things. None of my hybrids are here, though."

I gave her a puzzled look. "How do you know?"

She smiled. "It's kind of my thing. You know, to know things."

I ignored her and pushed past her to walk farther into the warehouse. I turned a corner and saw a dark wooden chair with a piece of paper folded on it.

I watched Seraphina and then my dad as he walked up to the chair to read the note.

He read it to himself and then read it out loud.

"Only one of us will leave here alive. You or me. Find me if you can, Mason." And it was signed, "Malute".

XLIV

Seraphina's eyes were now lit up with frustration. "I'm so sick of this guy and his games."

She snatched the note from my dad, read it and then shouted, "Malute, Malute, come out wherever you are!"

The train-like noise that haunted my dreams suddenly blared off.

His deep, raspy voice came from a distance. "Seraphina, how dare you come here and speak my name! You are a disgrace! I should have never blessed you with my blood!"

She jerked her head around, looking for him. "Why don't you come out and talk to me about this in person? Like a big boy?"

The train-like sound blared off again and nearly knocked me off my feet. My dad held me up.

"Mason, are you alright?"

"Ye-yeah. I'm fine."

Malute's voice broke up our conversation. "Mason, your dad does not belong in this realm. He belongs to the spirit world. You have shattered the balance of both worlds."

My dad's face tensed up. "Malute, I am going to kill you!"

Blinding lights flooded the room as the deafening sound went off again.

"I would love to see you try!" Malute roared.

I felt myself being pulled towards another room of the warehouse and I followed my instinct. As I got closer to the room, the familiar vibrations from my Sheer mist started running through my body.

I suddenly felt as if my entire body was on fire. My hands were clenched into tight fists and I slowly released them.

The rainbow mist slowly poured out and drifted off to the staircase that led to the second floor. I followed the mist as Seraphina and my dad followed a few steps behind me, in awe.

When we reached the second floor, the mist slowly started to retract back into my palms. I looked up and felt the hairs on the back of my neck stand up.

Malute was standing no more than fifty feet in front of me.

XLV.

His menacing grin kept me frozen in place but Seraphina walked past me.

"Malute, I'm so happy to see you. Let's cut to the chase, shall we? Where are my hybrids?"

Malute's focus stayed on me as he raised his hand and swung it to the side. Seraphina went flying through the air and hit the brick wall nearest to her.

"Mason, I see you have been keeping my little science experiment company. Thank you for returning her to me. She's been quite the nuisance since joining your company."

I stayed quiet, taking in his tall stature.

He continued, "I'm glad that you were able to reunite with your dad, even if it was only for a short period. Still, it's the quality not the quantity that counts. I'm sure you agree."

I turned around and saw that Malute had trapped the two of us behind one of his wards. My dad was standing next to Seraphina's limp body.

Malute made a clicking sound with his mouth, "No, sorry, they can't help you in here. You see, I've come to the realization that as long as you are alive, I will not be able to fully execute any of my plans."

I clenched my hands into fists and felt the mist begin to boil from the bottom of my feet.

He smiled at me. "Oh, Mason, you've come such a long way, and you've learned so much. Before, you were stronger than me because you thought you had your ancestors' help. I gather from your short time in the spirit realm, you know that they are no longer loyal to you or your family."

I mumbled, "What do they get out of helping you? What did you promise them?"

"I promised them eternal life, in this realm."

"That's not possible."

He started to slowly pace around me. "Oh, my dear boy, it is very possible. Why don't you look around?"

I looked behind him and saw that shadows started to surround the ward.

He continued, "You see, when you brought your dad back, you cracked the code. You did exactly what they and I needed you to do."

The shadows around the ward started to take shape, when I saw her. The tall blonde woman from the spirit realm was waving and smiling at me with sharp razor-like teeth.

Malute laughed when the other shadows followed the blonde woman and ran out of the room.

"Ah, it looks like my new step-children are going to have some fun in the city tonight."

"How are they here? What are they?"

He shook his finger back and forth. "No, no, Mason. You don't get to ask me any more questions."

He lifted his hands and a large, shadow orb began to build between his palms.

I closed my eyes and immediately felt the vibrations from my mist begin to run through my body.

I looked at my hands that were above my head and saw that there was a large, silver ball of light between them.

His smile seemed to turn into a kind of grimace right before he threw the orb at me.

I jumped a couple of feet to my left and then immediately threw my silver ball of light at him.

He dodged it and before he could throw another orb at me, I started to throw my silver orbs at his ward.

He shouted, "What do you think you are doing?"

"No, No, Malute! You don't get to ask me any more questions!"

I continued to dodge his orbs and throw my own at his wards until I saw it. A crack that was large enough for me to slide through.

The train-like sound went off and Malute was suddenly less than a foot in front of me. He grabbed me by the neck and lifted me up, high above his head.

I heard my dad shouting from outside of the ward. "Stop! put him down!"

Malute looked into my eyes and as I felt the life slowly start to drain out of me, Malute and I went flying across the floor.

I started to gasp as I tried to catch my breath. I looked up to see my friends all trying to break through the ward.

I stood up and raised my hands into the air. I opened my palms and the familiar rainbow mist went flying from my palm, towards the dark walls of the ward.

XLVI.

An explosion went off as the ward started to crumble from top to bottom. I wiped my eyes and saw my friends starting to get up.

I turned back around and saw Malute's eyes were glowing, eerily similar to Seraphina's.

Before he could say anything I opened my hands, palm up, and let the rainbow mist flood out of them. The mist surrounded him and his look turned from angry to confused.

As the mist closed him into a smaller area, I closed my palms to tighten the mist. His eyes dimmed and now, he looked scared.

"What, what is happening?"

I pulled the mist in tighter.

"You have always underestimated me. I have always been stronger than you."

His face was now pale as he hissed out, "You cannot kill me, you fool!"

I pulled the mist even tighter to prevent him from talking now. I walked towards him as the rainbow mist now surrounded his entire body with the exception of his eyes.

"I have always been stronger than you because I have people who actually love me."

I turned around and saw all of my friends, ready to attack. I smiled at them and then faced him again.

"You're right, I can't kill you. But I can banish you. I am banishing you from this realm and the spirit realm."

His eyeballs looked as if they were going to pop out at any moment.

I continued, "I am banishing you for everyone you've ever hurt. For my mom, for Mr. Wrightpress, for Darcy, for the Smithwick brothers and for the defenseless mundanes."

I shouted, "May the night hide you. May the light show you the way. May the mood guide you. And may the shadows forever hold our secrets. Malute, you are hereby banished!"

I clapped my hands together and the rainbow mist exploded into the air. The train-like sound blared off and the ground beneath my feet began to shake.

I looked at my group of friends who stared at me, stunned and then Tyler screamed out, "Dude, we've got to get out of here!"

XLVII.

The second we got outside the warehouse slowly collapsed to the ground. We all watched in silence as the dust began to settle.

"Mason, how did you do that?" Seraphina asked.

Everyone's attention was now on me. "I don't know. I don't know what I did. Isn't it your thing, to know things?"

Mackenna and Layla started to giggle when Benjy asked, "Mason, how did you know that using the council scripture would banish him?"

"I didn't know. Something just took over me. It's like I knew deep inside what I had to do."

My dad put his hand on my shoulder and let out a whistle. "I would hate to be on your bad side, son."

I smiled at him and Ty added, "Yeah, my best friend is a total badass! Holy crap! Mason, dude! Do you see what you did?"

He pointed at the lot where the warehouse had been standing just a few minutes earlier. Now there was just a huge heap of rubble.

I shrugged. "When y'all came inside, did y'all see anyone run out of the building?"

They all looked at each other, confused. Aden questioned, "Were we supposed to see someone leave the building?"

I stayed quiet and my dad answered for me. "Uh, when Mason was trapped in the ward with Malute, these shadow figures started to appear."

Seraphina huffed. "They weren't some mysterious shadows. They were y'alls little ancestors from the other side."

She pointed at my dad, Benjy, Ashton, Aden and I. "Yeah, your little back-stabbers somehow broke out of the spirt realm jail."

Jayland spoke for the first time since running out of the warehouse. "You mean to tell me, the Sheers that were helping Malute are now in this realm, running free?"

"That's exactly what I'm saying."

"You've got to be kidding me! I thought we were going to be able to go home now!" Mackenna moaned.

I wiped the sweat from my face and said, "Yeah, it looks like bringing my dad back caused a little bit of trouble."

Casey mumbled, "You've got to be kidding me."

I pulled the car keys out of my pocket and turned to my friends.

"Let's go find these traders and give them a one-way ticket to hell."

Tyler was the first person at my side. He put his hand on my shoulder, smiled and then said, "Let's do this, dude."

Mackenna, Benjy and Geoffrey were soon at our sides.

Geoffrey added, "God, I can't wait for all of this hunting down and tracking to be over with. I need a vacation."

Mackenna teased, "Geoffrey, you hardly ever lift a finger. You're practically on vacation all the time."

We all laughed and I looked up to see Layla standing in front of me.

She grabbed my hands and then looked into my eyes. "Mason, you are the bravest guy I've ever known. Let's send these back-stabbers to hell where they belong."

I squeezed her hands, leaned in and kissed her. "I love you, Lay."

"I love you too, Mason Connor Fitzgerald."

*

The third and final installment of the
Southern Secrets trilogy, Southern
Redemption, will be available soon.
Sign up for Abel's newsletter & get a FREE
book!
http://abelozuna.com/newsletter

* * *

Visit http://abelozuna.com/sscharacters for a
full Southern Secrets character list.

* * *

Follow Abel on social media:
Twitter: http://twitter.com/abelozuna4
Facebook: http://facebook.com/abelozuna04
Instagram: http://instagram.com/abelozuna4
Snapchat: abeloiv